The Role (
Vatica.
IN WWII
The untold Stories

Copyright © 2024 EVERLEAF BOOKS
All rights reserved.

INDEX

Introduction .... v – ix

Chapter 1 .... 1 - 5
Chapter 2 .... 6 - 10
Chapter 3 .... 11 - 14
Chapter 4 .... 15 - 20
Chapter 5 .... 21 - 25

Chapter 6 .... 26 - 30

Chapter 7 .... 31 - 34

Chapter 8 .... 35 - 38

Chapter 9 .... 39 - 43

Chapter 10 .... 44 - 47

Chapter 11 .... 48 - 51

Chapter 12 .... 52 - 55

Chapter 13 .... 56 - 59

Chapter 14 .... 60 - 63

Preface

In the annals of World War II, the role of the Vatican is a subject shrouded in both fascination and controversy. As the moral and spiritual center for millions of Catholics worldwide, the Vatican found itself at the heart of the deadliest conflict in human history, navigating treacherous political waters while facing profound ethical dilemmas. This book, *The Role of the Vatican in WWII*, seeks to explore the Vatican's complex position during the war, the choices made by its leaders, and the lasting impact of these decisions on the Church, world diplomacy, and historical memory.

At the center of this narrative stands Pope Pius XII, a figure both revered and criticized for his wartime actions—or perceived inaction. The Vatican's approach to diplomacy, particularly its efforts to maintain neutrality, broker peace, and preserve the rights of the Church in territories occupied by the Axis powers, will be explored in depth. Yet, the Church's stance during the Holocaust, often defined by its silence in the face of Nazi atrocities, raises some of the most profound moral questions this book aims to address.

This work does not seek to pass judgment but rather to provide a balanced account of the Vatican's multifaceted role during WWII. From the secretive negotiations with both the Axis and Allied powers to the behind-the-scenes efforts to save Jewish lives, the book highlights the Vatican's struggle to uphold its spiritual mission while contending with the harsh realities of global conflict.

As we turn the pages of history, the moral and political complexities faced by the Vatican during WWII continue to offer lessons for modern times. This book invites readers to engage with these complexities and reflect on how faith, power, and diplomacy intersected in one of the darkest chapters of human history.

Introduction
The Vatican's Unique Position During WWII

During World War II, the Vatican occupied a unique position—one of profound moral, political, and diplomatic influence. As the smallest sovereign state in the world, the Vatican had no military force or territorial ambitions, yet its significance extended far beyond its physical boundaries. At the helm of the Vatican was Pope Pius XII, whose leadership would shape the Church's response to one of the darkest periods in modern history.

The Vatican's role was paradoxical: it was an institution of peace in a world at war. Though geographically located within Italy, an Axis power, the Vatican sought to remain neutral in the conflict, attempting to serve as a moral compass and diplomatic intermediary. This neutrality, however, would become a subject of controversy and scrutiny as the war unfolded. Many argued that the Vatican's silence on certain atrocities—most notably the Holocaust—was a moral failing, while others contended that this very silence allowed the Vatican to act behind the scenes, saving countless lives through clandestine efforts.

The Vatican's unique status as a religious entity also meant that it held sway not just over political leaders, but over millions of Catholics worldwide. Its moral authority, wielded by the Pope, carried great weight in both Axis and Allied nations. Throughout the war, the Vatican used this influence to promote peace and negotiate humanitarian efforts, while also navigating the treacherous political landscape of totalitarian regimes, occupied territories, and resistance movements. The challenges of balancing moral leadership with diplomatic pragmatism would define the Vatican's complex role throughout the war.

Moreover, the Vatican had to contend with the internal pressures from the global Catholic community. In countries like Germany, France, and Poland, where the Catholic Church held significant sway, the local clergy and laity looked to Rome for guidance. Yet, the

Vatican's ability to publicly condemn or support certain actions was limited by its delicate diplomatic standing and the risk of retaliation against Catholics living under Axis control. This constant balancing act—between taking a moral stand and safeguarding the lives of millions of believers—contributed to the Vatican's enigmatic and sometimes criticized approach to the war.

Background on the Vatican's Influence in International Affairs

The Vatican has a long history of involvement in international affairs, dating back to its formation as a political entity. The Papal States, which existed from the 8th century until 1870, gave the Pope not only spiritual authority but also temporal power over large swathes of Italy. However, following the unification of Italy, the Vatican's territorial holdings were reduced to the small enclave that it occupies today—Vatican City. Despite this diminishment of its physical domain, the Vatican continued to wield considerable influence on the global stage through its religious authority and diplomatic network.

In the early 20th century, the Vatican had become a recognized sovereign entity through the Lateran Treaty of 1929, signed between the Holy See and the Kingdom of Italy under Mussolini's regime. This agreement gave the Vatican formal independence, allowing it to conduct diplomatic relations with nations across the world. By the time World War II erupted, the Vatican maintained diplomatic ties with both Axis and Allied nations, enabling it to act as a mediator, even as it struggled to maintain strict neutrality.

The Vatican's influence in international affairs was rooted in its ability to communicate directly with world leaders, and its vast network of bishops and clergy in every corner of the globe provided valuable intelligence. Vatican envoys were in regular contact with governments, military officials, and resistance movements, often passing messages that could not be sent through formal diplomatic channels. This access to information, combined with the Vatican's moral authority, made it an influential—but often unseen—player in global politics.

Moreover, the Vatican's consistent calls for peace, even in the face of aggressive war rhetoric from both sides, underscored its unique position as a global advocate for diplomacy over violence. Popes throughout history had consistently tried to mediate conflicts, and Pope Pius XII's Vatican was no different, though the challenges of WWII would push this tradition to its limits. Despite its desire for peace, the Vatican would find itself caught between the political realities of war and its mission to safeguard human life and spiritual well-being.

Overview of the Church's Historical Stance on War and Peace

The Catholic Church's stance on war and peace is deeply rooted in its theological teachings, which have evolved over centuries. Traditionally, the Church has promoted peace, viewing war as a last resort only to be waged under strict conditions. This is embodied in the doctrine of "Just War," which dates back to the writings of St. Augustine in the 4th century and was later elaborated upon by St. Thomas Aquinas in the Middle Ages.

The "Just War" theory outlines specific criteria under which war could be morally justified, such as the need for a legitimate authority to declare war, the necessity of a just cause, the use of war as a last resort, and the assurance that the war's outcomes would lead to more good than harm. These principles formed the moral framework by which the Church assessed conflicts throughout history, including the two World Wars of the 20th century.

Despite this framework, the Church has always preferred peace. Various popes throughout history have acted as mediators in conflicts, issuing encyclicals and making public calls for the cessation of violence. For instance, during World War I, Pope Benedict XV made repeated efforts to broker peace, issuing his famous 1917 Peace Note that called for an end to hostilities. Though largely ignored by the warring powers, it reflected the Church's long-standing commitment to diplomacy over bloodshed.

In the context of World War II, Pope Pius XII inherited this tradition of peacemaking. He began his papacy in 1939 with an encyclical, *Summi Pontificatus*, which emphasized the unity of mankind and called for peace among nations. However, as the war escalated, Pius XII found himself constrained by the practicalities of Vatican diplomacy and the sheer brutality of the global conflict. His reluctance to openly condemn the Axis powers—particularly Nazi Germany—led to accusations that the Church was not doing enough to oppose the evils of the war, particularly the Holocaust.

The Church's historical stance on war and peace thus became a crucial factor in how the Vatican responded to World War II. The conflict between adhering to the principles of "Just War" and the practicalities of war-time diplomacy created moral complexities that would define the Vatican's role throughout the war.

A Roadmap of the Vatican's WWII Role

The Vatican's involvement in World War II can be understood through three main lenses: diplomacy, humanitarian efforts, and moral controversy. This book will explore each of these aspects in depth, revealing the complex nature of Vatican policy and action during this period.

1. **Diplomacy**: The Vatican's diplomatic efforts during WWII were extensive. Pope Pius XII and his diplomats engaged in secret negotiations with both Axis and Allied powers, attempting to mediate and bring an end to hostilities. The Vatican's attempts at peace were often shrouded in secrecy, partly due to the delicate nature of its position, but also because of the need to maintain relations with regimes that were actively persecuting Catholics, Jews, and other minorities.
2. **Humanitarian Efforts**: Despite its criticized silence on the Holocaust, the Vatican was actively involved in saving lives. Through its network of monasteries, churches, and Catholic

organizations, the Vatican provided shelter to Jews, political refugees, and prisoners of war. These efforts, while often underreported, demonstrated the Vatican's commitment to human dignity and the protection of life during a time of unprecedented global violence.

3. **Moral Controversy**: Perhaps the most contentious aspect of the Vatican's role during WWII is the moral ambiguity surrounding its actions—or inactions. Pope Pius XII's decision not to publicly condemn Nazi atrocities has led to a lasting debate about whether the Vatican prioritized diplomacy over morality. Critics argue that the Church's silence amounted to complicity, while defenders claim that the Vatican's quiet diplomacy saved lives. This book will explore these moral dilemmas, offering a balanced view of the Vatican's difficult position during the war.

Through these themes, we will uncover the full complexity of the Vatican's wartime role—one that was marked by both quiet heroism and moral ambiguity. As the war raged across Europe and beyond, the Vatican stood as a beacon of peace, yet its actions—or lack thereof—have left a legacy that continues to spark debate. The following chapters will delve into the specifics of these themes, offering a comprehensive examination of the Vatican's place in the history of World War II.

Chapter 1: The Vatican and World Politics Before WWII

The Lateran Treaty (1929) and the Creation of the Vatican City as a Sovereign Entity

In 1929, the Vatican entered a new chapter in its political history with the signing of the Lateran Treaty, a pivotal agreement that established Vatican City as an independent and sovereign state. The treaty was the culmination of decades of tension between the Catholic Church and the Italian state, particularly following Italy's unification in the 19th century, which had stripped the Church of the Papal States and severely limited its territorial influence.

The Lateran Treaty was signed by representatives of the Holy See and the Italian government, specifically by Cardinal Pietro Gasparri for Pope Pius XI and Benito Mussolini for the Kingdom of Italy. The treaty resolved what had been known as the "Roman Question," a longstanding dispute over the Pope's role in temporal governance after the unification of Italy in 1870. In the years between the unification and the signing of the treaty, the Vatican had largely remained isolated from formal political affairs, rejecting the authority of the Italian state over the Papal States. This period, often referred to as the "self-imposed exile" of the Pope, ended with the Lateran Treaty.

The Lateran Treaty had three major components:

1. **Recognition of Vatican City as an independent sovereign state**: This granted the Pope full territorial sovereignty over the Vatican, a tiny enclave within Rome, covering only 44 hectares (110 acres). The treaty ensured that the Vatican would be neutral in international relations, a stance it would maintain during World War II.
2. **Compensation for the loss of the Papal States**: The Italian government agreed to compensate the Vatican with a large sum

of money for the territories it had annexed in the 19th century. This payment was crucial in helping the Vatican reestablish its financial independence and maintain its global operations.
3. **Concordat between the Church and the Italian State**: This agreement regulated the relationship between the Italian government and the Catholic Church, particularly in matters such as religious education, marriage, and the role of the clergy. It also established Catholicism as the official religion of Italy, giving the Church significant influence over Italian society and politics.

The significance of the Lateran Treaty cannot be overstated. For the Vatican, it marked the restoration of its temporal authority, albeit on a much smaller scale than before. For Mussolini, the treaty was a political coup, solidifying his control over a Catholic population that had been ambivalent about the fascist regime. The agreement with the Vatican gave Mussolini an aura of legitimacy, both domestically and internationally, as it appeared to reconcile the Church with the modern Italian state.

Beyond its immediate impact on Italy, the Lateran Treaty also positioned the Vatican as a fully recognized international actor, free to engage in diplomacy on its own terms. This newfound independence allowed the Vatican to build diplomatic relationships across Europe and beyond, which would become crucial as the political landscape of Europe began to shift in the 1930s with the rise of totalitarian regimes.

However, the Lateran Treaty also placed the Vatican in a delicate position. While it had regained its sovereign status, it was surrounded by an increasingly authoritarian Italy under Mussolini, and its role in world politics would soon be tested as fascism and totalitarianism swept across Europe.

The Vatican's Early Diplomacy with Rising Fascist Regimes in Italy and Germany

The 1920s and 1930s saw the rise of fascist regimes across Europe, most notably in Italy and Germany. As these movements gained power, the Vatican faced the difficult task of navigating its diplomatic relationships with governments that, while outwardly supportive of traditional values and authority, often espoused ideologies that conflicted with Catholic teachings on human dignity, individual freedom, and social justice.

In Italy, the relationship between the Vatican and the fascist regime was complicated by the Lateran Treaty. Mussolini, having consolidated power by the mid-1920s, was eager to present his regime as a defender of traditional values, including the Church. The Vatican, for its part, saw an opportunity to secure the rights of the Church and protect its interests in a rapidly modernizing and secularizing society. While Pope Pius XI had reservations about Mussolini's dictatorship, the benefits of the Lateran Treaty—particularly the legal protections it offered the Church—encouraged a cautious diplomacy between the two powers.

Mussolini's fascist ideology emphasized the importance of a strong, centralized state, nationalism, and militarism, all of which clashed with the Church's teachings on social justice and the role of the family and community in society. However, Mussolini's regime was also staunchly anti-communist, a position that the Vatican shared. Communism, with its atheistic tenets and hostility toward religion, was seen as a direct threat to the Church. This common enemy led to a degree of cooperation between the Vatican and the fascist government, despite their ideological differences.

In Germany, the rise of Adolf Hitler and the Nazi Party in the early 1930s posed an even greater challenge for the Vatican. Hitler's government, like Mussolini's, portrayed itself as a defender of traditional values, and the Nazi regime initially sought to court the Catholic Church to solidify its support among the German populace. In 1933, shortly after Hitler came to power, the Vatican signed a concordat with

Nazi Germany, known as the Reichskonkordat, which regulated the Church's rights within the German state.

The Reichskonkordat was meant to protect the rights of Catholics and the autonomy of the Church in Germany, but it soon became clear that Hitler's regime had little intention of honoring the agreement. While the Vatican had hoped to secure the position of the Church within the Third Reich, the Nazis began a systematic campaign of undermining the Church's influence, particularly in areas such as education and youth organizations. Catholic priests and clergy were harassed, imprisoned, or worse, and the Nazi regime promoted a form of "Positive Christianity" that sought to strip Christianity of its Jewish roots and align it with Nazi racial ideology.

The Vatican's diplomatic relations with Nazi Germany became increasingly strained throughout the 1930s. Pope Pius XI and his advisors were alarmed by the Nazis' anti-Semitism, racial policies, and attacks on Catholic institutions. The Pope issued a number of statements condemning aspects of Nazi ideology, most notably in his 1937 encyclical *Mit Brennender Sorge* (With Burning Concern), which criticized the regime's violations of the Reichskonkordat and its racial policies. The encyclical, which was smuggled into Germany and read aloud in churches, marked a clear public rebuke of the Nazi government, though it stopped short of outright condemnation of Hitler's regime as a whole.

This period of Vatican diplomacy was marked by a careful balancing act. The Vatican sought to protect the Church's interests and maintain influence in increasingly authoritarian states, while also upholding its moral teachings. The growing power of fascist regimes in Italy and Germany presented profound challenges, and the Vatican's cautious diplomacy during this time laid the groundwork for its controversial role in World War II.

Pope Pius XI's Cautious Stance Toward Nazism and Fascism

Pope Pius XI, who led the Catholic Church from 1922 until his death in 1939, faced the daunting task of responding to the rise of totalitarian ideologies in Europe. His papacy was marked by an increasing tension between the Vatican's diplomatic efforts and its moral teachings, particularly as fascism and Nazism began to reshape the political landscape of Europe.

From the outset, Pius XI was deeply concerned about the growing influence of fascism, both in Italy and abroad. While he signed the Lateran Treaty with Mussolini, he remained wary of the fascist regime's disregard for individual freedoms and its aggressive nationalism. Throughout the 1930s, Pius XI increasingly expressed his discomfort with Mussolini's policies, particularly as the regime began to align more closely with Nazi Germany. The passage of Italy's racial laws in 1938, which mirrored Germany's anti-Semitic legislation, further alienated the Pope from Mussolini's government.

Pius XI's relationship with Nazi Germany was even more fraught. While the Vatican had hoped that the 1933 Reichskonkordat would protect the rights of Catholics in Germany, it quickly became clear that the Nazi regime had no intention of respecting the agreement. The Pope was particularly disturbed by the Nazis' racial ideology, which he saw as fundamentally incompatible with Christian teachings. In 1937, he issued the encyclical *Mit Brennender Sorge*, which condemned the Nazi regime's violation of the concordat, its racial policies, and its promotion of a distorted version of Christianity.

The encyclical was a bold move, especially given the Vatican's tradition of cautious diplomacy. It was written in German, rather than Latin, to ensure that it could be read directly by the German people, and it was smuggled into the country to be read aloud in churches. *Mit Brennender Sorge* represented one of the strongest public condemnations of Nazi ideology by the Vatican prior to World War II. However, it was also indicative of the Pope's careful approach—while the encyclical criticized aspects of the Nazi regime, it did not call for outright opposition to Hitler or his government.

Pope Pius XI's cautious stance toward fascism and Nazism was shaped by several factors. First, he was deeply committed to maintaining the independence and influence of the Church in an increasingly hostile political environment. He believed that diplomacy and dialogue, rather than confrontation, would allow the Vatican to protect its interests and those of Catholics across Europe. Second, the Pope was acutely aware of the threat posed by communism, particularly in the Soviet Union. Like Mussolini and Hitler, Pius XI saw communism as a direct threat to Christianity, and this shared enemy complicated the Vatican's relations with fascist regimes.

Despite these challenges, Pius XI remained steadfast in his belief that the Church could not compromise its moral teachings, even in the face of political pressure. His papacy was characterized by a careful balance between diplomacy and moral authority, and his legacy would shape the Vatican's approach to World War II under his successor, Pope Pius XII.

Chapter 2: The Early Days of War (1939-1940)

The Election of Pope Pius XII in 1939 and the Significance of His Background

In March 1939, Cardinal Eugenio Pacelli was elected as Pope Pius XII, a pivotal figure whose leadership would define the Vatican's role during World War II. His election came at a critical moment, just months before the outbreak of the war, and his personal background significantly influenced the Vatican's diplomatic approach in the early days of the conflict.

Pius XII was no stranger to the complexities of European diplomacy. Before becoming pope, Pacelli had served as the Vatican's Secretary of State and had a long diplomatic career within the Holy See. He had been the papal nuncio (ambassador) to Germany during the Weimar Republic and had negotiated the Reichskonkordat with Nazi Germany in 1933. His firsthand experience with German politics and his deep understanding of European affairs made him a natural choice to lead the Vatican through the turbulent times ahead.

One of the most significant aspects of Pius XII's background was his deep commitment to diplomacy. As a skilled diplomat, he had spent years building relationships with both Axis and Allied powers, trying to safeguard the interests of the Catholic Church in increasingly hostile environments. This diplomatic experience shaped his approach to the war. Unlike his predecessor, Pius XI, who had been more outspoken in his condemnation of Nazism, Pius XII was determined to maintain a position of neutrality, believing that the Vatican's primary role was to act as a mediator and peacemaker rather than take sides in the conflict.

The significance of Pius XII's election also lay in his vision for the Church's role in global politics. He believed that the Church should remain above political struggles, serving as a moral authority and a voice for peace in a world increasingly driven by ideology and violence. His election marked a shift in Vatican strategy, with a stronger emphasis on diplomacy, behind-the-scenes negotiations, and a cautious approach to public statements on the war.

Despite his diplomatic inclinations, Pius XII's election was met with concern in some quarters. Many feared that his past dealings with Nazi Germany, particularly his role in the Reichskonkordat, indicated that he would be too accommodating to the Axis powers. Others, particularly in the Allied nations, hoped that his extensive experience in European diplomacy would make him a valuable ally in their fight against totalitarianism. These conflicting expectations placed Pius XII in a delicate position as the war began.

Initial Vatican Neutrality and Its Emphasis on Peace

As the clouds of war loomed over Europe in 1939, the Vatican, under the newly elected Pope Pius XII, adopted a stance of strict neutrality. This neutrality was grounded in the belief that the Church's primary mission was to be a beacon of peace, offering moral guidance rather than becoming entangled in the political and military struggles of the world's powers.

The Vatican's official position was clear: it sought to remain above the conflict, refraining from taking sides, and focusing on humanitarian efforts and peace mediation. Pius XII, in his first encyclical *Summi Pontificatus*, issued in October 1939, just after the outbreak of the war, emphasized the Church's call for peace and the importance of Christian unity in the face of war. The encyclical condemned the invasion of Poland and the violence of the conflict, but it carefully avoided directly blaming any one nation for the war. Instead, Pius XII focused on the broader moral crisis facing Europe and the need for reconciliation and mutual understanding.

In *Summi Pontificatus*, Pius XII lamented the collapse of Christian civilization in the face of nationalism, totalitarianism, and militarism. He called for the restoration of Christian values in Europe, urging leaders and nations to turn away from the destructive forces that had led to war. However, his call for peace was carefully worded to maintain neutrality. While he condemned the war itself, he refrained from explicitly condemning the Axis powers or calling for armed resistance against them.

Pope Pius XII's neutrality was not simply a matter of principle; it was also a practical necessity. The Vatican was a small, independent state surrounded by Fascist Italy and closely watched by Nazi Germany. Any overt alignment with the Allies could have jeopardized the Vatican's ability to function, placing its institutions and its population of clergy, refugees, and diplomats at risk. Moreover, Pius XII believed that if the Vatican remained neutral, it could serve as a mediator between the warring parties and act as a channel for peace negotiations, which might be impossible if it appeared to favor one side over the other.

This stance of neutrality was not without controversy. Critics, particularly in the Allied nations, accused the Vatican of moral cowardice, arguing that its refusal to condemn Nazism and fascism outright gave legitimacy to these regimes. In particular, Pius XII's failure to speak out more forcefully against the persecution of Jews and other minorities during the early stages of the war raised concerns about the Vatican's priorities. Many felt that the Church had a moral obligation to take a stronger stand against the atrocities being committed by the Axis powers.

Despite these criticisms, Pius XII's emphasis on peace and neutrality remained steadfast. He believed that by staying out of the conflict, the Vatican could maintain its moral authority and continue to serve as a voice for reconciliation and humanity. Throughout the early days of the war, the Pope issued several public statements calling for an end to the violence and urging leaders to seek peaceful solutions to their disputes. However, these appeals often fell on deaf ears, as the war escalated and the major powers became increasingly entrenched in their positions.

The Vatican's neutrality also allowed it to engage in humanitarian efforts during the war. The Pope worked behind the scenes to provide assistance to refugees, prisoners of war, and civilians caught in the conflict. The Vatican's diplomatic channels were used to facilitate communications between warring nations and to negotiate the release of prisoners and the protection of religious sites. These efforts, though largely hidden from public view, were a significant part of the Vatican's role during the early years of the war.

Early Diplomatic Exchanges Between the Vatican and European Governments

As the war unfolded in 1939 and 1940, the Vatican engaged in a flurry of diplomatic activity, seeking to position itself as a neutral mediator while also protecting the interests of the Catholic Church in Europe. Pius XII's diplomatic strategy was rooted in his belief that the Vatican could act as a bridge between the warring powers, using its unique position to facilitate peace talks and negotiations.

One of the key challenges the Vatican faced in its early diplomacy was maintaining open lines of communication with both Axis and Allied governments. Despite its neutrality, the Vatican had to navigate the competing demands and suspicions of these powers, each of which sought to influence the Church's stance on the war. The Vatican's diplomatic corps, led by Cardinal Luigi Maglione, Pius XII's Secretary of State, worked tirelessly to maintain contacts with both sides, often acting as intermediaries for messages between governments that were otherwise in direct conflict.

In its dealings with the Axis powers, the Vatican maintained cautious but open relations with both Germany and Italy. Despite the growing evidence of Nazi atrocities, particularly against Jews and other minorities, the Vatican refrained from publicly condemning the German government during the early days of the war. Instead, it sought to use quiet diplomacy to mitigate the worst excesses of the Nazi regime. This included efforts to secure the release of Catholic clergy imprisoned by the Nazis and to protect Catholic institutions in occupied territories.

At the same time, the Vatican worked to maintain its relationship with the Allied powers, particularly the United States and Great Britain. Both nations viewed the Vatican as a potentially valuable ally in their struggle against the Axis, though they were often frustrated by its refusal to take a more overtly anti-Nazi stance. British diplomats, in particular, pressed the Vatican to issue stronger condemnations of Hitler's regime, but Pius XII remained committed to his policy of neutrality.

One of the most significant diplomatic efforts during this period was the Vatican's attempt to broker peace between the warring nations. In late 1939 and early 1940, Pius XII made several quiet overtures to European leaders, proposing the possibility of peace talks. These efforts, however, were largely unsuccessful. The rapid escalation of the war, including Germany's invasion of Poland and the subsequent declarations of war by Britain and France, made any hopes of early peace increasingly unrealistic.

Despite these setbacks, the Vatican continued to use its diplomatic channels to advocate for humanitarian causes. In particular, Pius XII worked to provide assistance to displaced persons and refugees, many of whom sought sanctuary within Vatican City or in Church-run institutions across Europe. The Vatican's diplomatic corps played a key role in facilitating these efforts, working with both Axis and Allied governments to secure safe passage for refugees and to ensure the protection of religious sites and personnel in war zones.

Chapter 3: Vatican Diplomacy with the Axis Powers

Relationships with Mussolini's Italy

The Vatican's diplomatic relationship with Fascist Italy under Benito Mussolini was complex, deeply influenced by the Lateran Treaty of 1929, which had established Vatican City as a sovereign state and resolved longstanding tensions between the Catholic Church and the Italian government. Despite this formal agreement, tensions simmered beneath the surface, especially as Mussolini's regime became more authoritarian and aligned itself with Adolf Hitler's Nazi Germany.

The Lateran Treaty, negotiated during the reign of Pope Pius XI, had granted the Vatican independence and financial compensation for the Papal States lost in the 19th century. It also established Catholicism as the state religion of Italy. This agreement provided the Vatican with political security, but it also came with strings attached. Mussolini, eager to consolidate power, used the Church's backing to legitimize his regime and portray himself as a defender of Italian Catholic values. The Vatican, for its part, saw the treaty as a way to protect the Church's influence in Italy, but this delicate balance would be tested as Mussolini's Fascism took a more militaristic and nationalistic turn in the 1930s.

By the time World War II began, the Vatican's relationship with Mussolini had become strained. Pope Pius XII, who succeeded Pius XI in 1939, was more cautious about publicly engaging with Mussolini's regime than his predecessor. While he sought to maintain the Vatican's position as a neutral mediator in the conflict, the increasingly repressive policies of the Italian Fascist state, particularly its alignment with Nazi Germany, created significant moral and political dilemmas for the Vatican.

Mussolini's introduction of anti-Semitic laws in 1938, modeled on Germany's Nuremberg Laws, marked a turning point in Vatican-Italian relations. These laws targeted Italy's Jewish population, stripping them of civil rights, banning intermarriage, and excluding Jews from public life. The Vatican, though privately critical of these measures, chose not to issue a strong public condemnation at the time, in part to preserve its diplomatic standing with the Italian government.

Pius XII, while maintaining open lines of communication with Mussolini, engaged in behind-the-scenes efforts to mitigate the worst effects of Fascist policies on Catholics and other vulnerable groups. Vatican diplomats worked quietly to secure the release of prisoners and protect the rights of Catholics who were being persecuted under Fascist rule. However, these efforts were limited, as Mussolini was increasingly reliant on his alliance with Hitler, and the Fascist regime's policies became more aligned with Nazi ideology.

The Vatican also faced the challenge of navigating Italy's role in the war. Mussolini's decision to join forces with Nazi Germany and Japan in the Axis alliance placed Italy in direct opposition to the Allied powers, many of which had significant Catholic populations. This created a diplomatic tightrope for the Vatican, as it sought to maintain neutrality while also safeguarding the interests of Catholics in Italy and abroad.

Despite these challenges, the Vatican's relationship with Italy remained diplomatically cordial, largely due to the Lateran Treaty, which Mussolini had no interest in jeopardizing. The Pope's cautious diplomacy with Italy reflected the broader strategy of Vatican neutrality during the early stages of the war, as Pius XII sought to position the Church as a voice for peace, even as Europe descended into chaos.

Vatican Diplomacy in Nazi Germany: Trying to Maintain Church Rights Under Totalitarianism

The Vatican's relationship with Nazi Germany was fraught with difficulties from the outset. The 1933 Reichskonkordat, signed by the Vatican and the Nazi regime, was intended to secure the rights of the

Catholic Church in Germany, but it quickly became clear that Hitler's government had no intention of honoring the agreement in good faith. The Vatican, under Pope Pius XII, found itself in a delicate position, trying to protect the Church's rights in Germany while navigating the growing totalitarianism of the Nazi state.

The Reichskonkordat, negotiated when Pius XII was still Cardinal Eugenio Pacelli, was initially seen as a victory for the Church. It guaranteed the Church's autonomy in education, religious services, and the appointment of clergy, in exchange for the Vatican agreeing not to interfere in German political affairs. However, almost immediately after the concordat was signed, the Nazi regime began to violate its terms. Catholic organizations were disbanded, clergy were harassed and imprisoned, and Catholic schools were pressured to conform to Nazi ideology.

Pius XII, now pope, was acutely aware of the dangers posed by the Nazi regime. His experience as nuncio to Germany had given him insight into Hitler's ambitions and the ideological extremism of the Nazis. Nevertheless, the Vatican was reluctant to openly confront the Nazi government, fearing that doing so would result in even harsher reprisals against the Church and its followers in Germany. Instead, Pius XII pursued a policy of quiet diplomacy, attempting to protect the Church's interests through behind-the-scenes negotiations with Nazi officials.

This diplomatic strategy was not without its critics. Many within the Church, particularly in Germany, felt that the Vatican was not doing enough to resist Nazi oppression. Catholic bishops and priests in Germany often found themselves caught between the demands of the Nazi state and their loyalty to the Vatican. Some clergy, like Bishop Clemens von Galen, became outspoken critics of Nazi policies, particularly the regime's euthanasia program, but the Vatican remained cautious in its public statements.

Despite the challenges, the Vatican did make some efforts to push back against Nazi encroachments on Church rights. In 1940, the Holy

See issued a series of protests to the German government, objecting to the closure of Catholic schools, the arrest of priests, and the suppression of Catholic publications. These protests, however, had little effect on the regime's policies.

One of the most significant concerns for the Vatican was the Nazi regime's attempt to replace traditional religious practices with its own brand of nationalist, racialist ideology. The Nazis promoted a distorted form of Christianity, known as *Positive Christianity*, which sought to purge the faith of its Jewish roots and align it with Nazi principles. This movement, which had the backing of some Nazi officials, posed a direct threat to the Catholic Church's teachings and its influence in German society.

The Vatican's response to these developments was cautious but firm. Pius XII and his diplomats worked to protect the Church's doctrinal integrity, issuing statements reaffirming traditional Catholic teachings and warning against the dangers of ideologies that sought to distort the faith. However, the Vatican's ability to directly challenge the Nazi regime was limited by the realities of totalitarianism, and much of its diplomatic work in Germany focused on protecting the rights of Catholics under increasingly repressive conditions.

Vatican Responses to Anti-Semitic Laws in Germany and Italy

The Vatican's response to the anti-Semitic laws enacted by both Nazi Germany and Fascist Italy during the early years of World War II was a deeply complex and controversial aspect of its wartime diplomacy. While the Vatican privately opposed the persecution of Jews, its public statements on the issue were often muted, reflecting its broader strategy of cautious neutrality and behind-the-scenes diplomacy.

In Nazi Germany, the introduction of the Nuremberg Laws in 1935 marked the beginning of a systematic effort to marginalize, disenfranchise, and ultimately exterminate the Jewish population. These laws prohibited intermarriage between Jews and non-Jews, stripped Jews of their citizenship, and laid the groundwork for the horrors of the Holocaust. The Vatican, under Pope Pius XI and later Pope Pius XII, was deeply concerned about these developments but refrained from issuing a direct public condemnation of the laws.

Behind the scenes, Vatican diplomats did express their opposition to Nazi racial policies. In 1937, Pope Pius XI issued the encyclical *Mit Brennender Sorge* (With Burning Concern), which condemned the Nazi regime's efforts to undermine the Church and its persecution of religious and ethnic minorities. The encyclical, written in German and secretly distributed in Germany, was a bold statement against Nazi ideology, but it did not specifically mention the Jews by name. Instead, it focused on broader moral and theological principles, condemning racism and the deification of the state.

Pope Pius XII, who succeeded Pius XI in 1939, continued this cautious approach. While he expressed sympathy for the victims of Nazi persecution, including Jews, his public statements were often carefully worded to avoid provoking the Nazis directly. Critics have argued that Pius XII's reluctance to speak out more forcefully against the Holocaust represented a moral failure, while others contend that the Vatican's behind-the-scenes efforts to assist Jews and other persecuted groups were significant but necessarily discreet.

In Italy, the introduction of anti-Semitic laws in 1938 under Mussolini's Fascist regime was similarly troubling for the Vatican. These laws, which mirrored the Nuremberg Laws, targeted Italy's small Jewish population, excluding them from public life and placing severe restrictions on their civil rights. The Vatican was deeply opposed to these laws, viewing them as a violation of human dignity and the Church's teachings on the equality of all people.

Pius XII's response to the Italian racial laws was more direct than his approach to Nazi Germany. In private meetings with Mussolini's representatives, the Pope protested the persecution of Jews and expressed concern about the impact of these policies on the Church's moral authority. The Vatican also worked to protect Jewish converts to Catholicism, ensuring that they were exempt from some of the more draconian measures of the racial laws.

However, like in Germany, the Vatican's public response to Italy's anti-Semitic laws was measured. While Church leaders in Italy, including Cardinal Schuster of Milan, condemned the laws from the pulpit, the Vatican itself stopped short of issuing an official condemnation. This cautious approach was largely driven by the Vatican's desire to maintain its diplomatic standing with Mussolini's regime and to avoid provoking a confrontation that could jeopardize the Church's ability to operate in Italy.

Chapter 4: The Vatican's Approach to Allied Powers

Vatican Neutrality and Relations with Britain and France

During the early years of World War II, the Vatican under Pope Pius XII maintained a position of strict neutrality, attempting to act as a moral voice above the political fray. The Vatican's neutral stance was meant to allow the Church to serve as a potential mediator in the conflict and to provide humanitarian assistance to victims on both sides. However, this neutrality was not without its complications, particularly in the Vatican's relations with Britain and France.

Before the war, the Vatican had longstanding diplomatic relations with both Britain and France. These countries were home to significant Catholic populations, and the Church had long played an important role in public and political life there. When World War II began in 1939, Britain and France were among the first to declare war on Nazi Germany after Hitler's invasion of Poland, positioning themselves as the main Western Allies. Despite their military and moral opposition to the Nazi regime, the Vatican maintained diplomatic channels with both countries while emphasizing its non-combatant role in the conflict.

Vatican neutrality in this context was, in part, a practical decision. Pope Pius XII believed that by staying out of the political and military alliances of the war, the Church could act as a peace broker. The Pope was deeply concerned about the destruction and moral degradation caused by war, and he sought to maintain the Vatican's moral authority as a neutral party. This position also allowed the Vatican to avoid retaliation from Axis powers, particularly Nazi Germany and Fascist Italy, both of which were hostile to Catholicism in varying degrees.

However, the Vatican's neutrality also meant that it refrained from openly supporting Britain and France in their fight against fascism, which drew criticism from some quarters. In private, the Vatican had a more favorable view of the Allied cause, particularly because Britain and France opposed the totalitarian ideologies of Nazi Germany and Mussolini's Italy. Yet, the Vatican's cautious diplomacy often gave the impression that it was unwilling to take a moral stand against the aggressors.

Pope Pius XII's position during the early stages of the war involved calling for peace and attempting to mediate between the warring nations. In 1939, he sent diplomatic letters to both the Axis and Allied governments, urging them to pursue a peaceful resolution to the conflict. The Vatican also made repeated attempts to broker ceasefires and peace talks, though these efforts were largely unsuccessful. Neither side was willing to consider negotiations, especially as the war escalated.

The Vatican's relations with Britain and France were further complicated by the changing dynamics of the war. In 1940, France fell to Nazi Germany, leading to the establishment of the Vichy regime, which collaborated with the Nazis. The Vatican maintained diplomatic relations with both the Vichy government and the Free French forces led by Charles de Gaulle. This dual diplomacy allowed the Vatican to retain some influence in occupied France, but it also led to accusations that the Church was legitimizing the Vichy regime's collaboration with the Nazis.

Despite these challenges, the Vatican's relationship with Britain remained largely positive throughout the war. British diplomats in Rome kept close contact with Vatican officials, and the British government appreciated the Vatican's humanitarian efforts, especially its work to aid prisoners of war and displaced civilians. However, Britain also hoped that the Vatican would take a stronger stance against Nazi Germany, particularly as evidence of the Holocaust began to emerge. The Vatican's cautious diplomacy, while aimed at preserving neutrality, sometimes frustrated British officials who wanted a more explicit condemnation of Nazi atrocities.

Diplomatic Connections with the United States: Cardinal Spellman and President Roosevelt

The Vatican's relationship with the United States during World War II was a crucial aspect of its wartime diplomacy. The U.S., led by President Franklin D. Roosevelt, emerged as a major power in the fight against the Axis, and the Vatican sought to maintain strong ties with Washington. One of the key figures in fostering this relationship was Cardinal Francis Spellman, the Archbishop of New York, who became a close confidant of both Pope Pius XII and President Roosevelt.

Cardinal Spellman played a central role in the Vatican's diplomatic efforts with the United States. Known for his political savvy and close connections with American leaders, Spellman acted as an unofficial liaison between the Vatican and the U.S. government. He frequently traveled to Rome to meet with the Pope and Vatican officials, carrying messages between the Holy See and Washington. His close relationship with President Roosevelt allowed him to advocate for Vatican concerns, particularly on issues related to the war and the post-war world order.

Roosevelt, for his part, was keen to maintain good relations with the Vatican. The United States, though a secular nation, had a large Catholic population, and Roosevelt recognized the importance of the Church's moral and humanitarian influence. In 1939, shortly after the outbreak of the war, Roosevelt appointed Myron C. Taylor as his personal representative to the Vatican, a move that helped strengthen diplomatic ties between the two states.

One of the key issues in the Vatican's relationship with the United States was the war's humanitarian crisis. The Vatican, through its diplomatic channels, urged the U.S. to take action to protect civilians and provide relief to refugees and displaced persons. The Holy See also worked closely with American Catholic organizations to coordinate aid for war-torn Europe. These efforts were particularly important in occupied territories, where the Vatican used its neutral status to negotiate the release of prisoners and protect vulnerable populations.

While Vatican-U.S. relations were largely positive, there were also tensions. Roosevelt's administration was concerned about the Vatican's neutrality, particularly in light of its dealings with Axis powers. Some American officials felt that the Vatican was too soft on Fascist Italy and Nazi Germany, especially when it came to addressing the persecution of Jews. These concerns were heightened as the war progressed and reports of the Holocaust began to reach the Vatican.

Nevertheless, the Vatican's diplomacy with the United States was an important aspect of its broader wartime strategy. Pius XII, through figures like Cardinal Spellman, sought to use his influence to shape the post-war order, advocating for peace and stability in Europe. The Pope also shared concerns with Roosevelt about the threat of Communism, which became a key issue in Vatican-U.S. relations as the war drew to a close.

How Vatican Concerns About Communism Influenced Its Views on the Western Allies

One of the most significant factors shaping the Vatican's view of the Western Allies during World War II was its deep concern about the spread of Communism. The Vatican had long been opposed to Communism, which it viewed as a threat to both religious freedom and the social order. Pope Pius XII, like his predecessors, was particularly worried about the influence of the Soviet Union, which was officially atheist and had persecuted religious institutions since the Bolshevik Revolution of 1917.

The Vatican's fear of Communism influenced its diplomatic approach to the Western Allies, particularly as the Soviet Union became a major player in the war following Germany's invasion in 1941. While the Vatican had initially welcomed the U.S. and Britain's efforts to combat Nazi Germany, it was increasingly concerned about the implications of an Allied victory that included the Soviet Union. Pius

XII worried that the defeat of the Axis could lead to the expansion of Soviet influence in Europe, particularly in Catholic countries like Poland, Hungary, and Italy.

These concerns shaped the Vatican's wartime diplomacy. While Pius XII remained neutral, he privately supported efforts to limit the spread of Communism. In 1942, for example, the Vatican welcomed the Allied invasion of North Africa, which was seen as a way to protect Catholic populations in the region from both Axis and Communist influence. Similarly, the Vatican was cautious in its dealings with the Soviet Union, despite the fact that the USSR was fighting alongside the Western Allies.

Pope Pius XII's anti-Communist stance also influenced his views on post-war Europe. The Vatican was deeply concerned about the future of Eastern Europe, where the Soviet Union was gaining control of several countries as it pushed back the Nazis. Pius XII feared that Soviet domination of these regions would lead to the suppression of the Catholic Church, as had already occurred in the Soviet Union itself. As a result, the Vatican lobbied the Western Allies to protect religious freedom in any post-war settlement.

The Vatican's anti-Communist position also brought it closer to the United States, particularly as the Cold War began to take shape toward the end of World War II. Pius XII viewed the U.S. as a bulwark against the spread of Communism and was eager to strengthen diplomatic ties with Washington. This shared concern about Communism would become a defining feature of Vatican-U.S. relations in the post-war era, as both the Holy See and the U.S. worked to contain Soviet influence in Europe and beyond

Chapter 5: The Vatican and the Holocaust – A Moral Dilemma

Pope Pius XII's Controversial Silence on the Jewish Holocaust

The Holocaust stands as one of the most horrific chapters in human history, marked by the systematic extermination of six million Jews and millions of others deemed undesirable by the Nazi regime. Within this tragic context, Pope Pius XII's silence regarding the Holocaust has generated significant debate and controversy. Critics argue that his failure to speak out forcefully against the atrocities constituted a moral failure, while defenders contend that he was limited by the complexities of wartime diplomacy.

Pope Pius XII ascended to the papacy in March 1939, just months before the outbreak of World War II. From the outset of the conflict, he adopted a policy of neutrality, aiming to position the Vatican as a moral authority above the fray. However, as the war progressed, and reports of mass killings of Jews began to surface, the Pope's silence became increasingly problematic.

Many historians and scholars have pointed to specific instances where Pope Pius XII could have spoken out more forcefully against the Holocaust. For example, in 1942, a significant report detailing the Nazi's extermination efforts reached the Vatican. This report came from the Polish government-in-exile, outlining the dire situation of Jews in occupied Europe. Yet, despite this information, the Pope refrained from making any public statements condemning the atrocities.

Critics argue that Pius XII's silence during such a pivotal moment represented a profound moral failure on the part of the Church. They contend that by not speaking out publicly, the Pope missed an opportunity to mobilize global opinion against the Holocaust and to urge nations to take action. This silence was compounded by the fact that many Catholic leaders and laypeople in occupied countries had already begun to resist Nazi policies and protect Jewish lives.

Defenders of Pius XII, on the other hand, argue that the Pope's position was dictated by the realities of wartime diplomacy. They assert that he feared that an outspoken denunciation of the Nazis might provoke retaliation against Catholics in occupied territories or disrupt the Vatican's humanitarian efforts. In their view, Pius XII sought to balance his moral convictions with the practical realities of a complex and dangerous political landscape.

Furthermore, some defenders contend that the Pope's silence should be understood in the context of the Vatican's broader efforts to negotiate peace and protect the Church's interests in Europe. They argue that Pius XII believed that a more measured approach could ultimately yield better results for the Church and for those suffering under Nazi rule. However, this perspective raises further ethical questions: does the potential for diplomatic effectiveness justify silence in the face of mass murder?

The controversy surrounding Pius XII's silence on the Holocaust continues to be a subject of intense debate among historians, theologians, and the public. Many believe that a more vocal condemnation could have galvanized resistance against the Nazi regime and perhaps saved lives. Others argue that the complexities of the time necessitated a more cautious approach. Ultimately, Pius XII's silence remains a profound moral dilemma, prompting reflections on the responsibilities of spiritual leaders in the face of atrocity.

Efforts by the Vatican to Secretly Save Jews: Sheltering Refugees, Issuing False Papers, and Behind-the-Scenes Efforts

While Pope Pius XII's public silence on the Holocaust has been widely criticized, it is essential to explore the Vatican's clandestine efforts to save Jews during this period. Despite the constraints of diplomacy and the risks involved, many Church officials, priests, and religious orders engaged in significant activities aimed at sheltering Jews and providing them with the means to escape Nazi persecution.

The Vatican itself became a refuge for many Jews fleeing the Holocaust. Under the auspices of various religious orders, such as the Jesuits and Franciscans, hundreds of Jewish refugees were hidden within convents, monasteries, and church buildings throughout Europe. These religious institutions provided not only shelter but also food and medical care to those in need. This underground network of support was crucial for many who faced imminent danger from the Nazis.

One of the most notable efforts to save Jewish lives involved the issuance of false baptismal certificates. Some Church officials took it upon themselves to create false documents, allowing Jews to pose as Catholics and thereby escape deportation. In many cases, these documents enabled Jews to evade Nazi scrutiny and access safe havens. While the Vatican officially discouraged such actions, individual clergy members often acted independently, driven by their moral convictions and a desire to save lives.

Additionally, the Vatican played a role in negotiating for the release of Jewish prisoners. Reports indicate that the Holy See sought to intercede with Axis governments, advocating for the release of those detained in concentration camps. Although these efforts were often limited in scope and effectiveness, they highlight the complex moral landscape in which the Vatican operated. Many of these negotiations were conducted behind closed doors, illustrating the tension between public neutrality and private action.

The Vatican's efforts to save Jews also extended to international diplomacy. The Holy See communicated with other nations, urging them to accept Jewish refugees and provide safe passage for those fleeing Europe. Although the Vatican faced numerous challenges in these endeavors, its diplomatic channels enabled it to advocate for Jewish lives in a context of widespread indifference and hostility.

While the efforts to save Jews were significant, they were not without controversy. Critics have argued that these actions were insufficient given the scale of the Holocaust. Many contend that the Vatican could have done more to mobilize international opinion and coordinate a larger-scale rescue operation. Furthermore, the secrecy surrounding these efforts has led some to question the moral integrity of the Vatican's approach.

Ultimately, the Vatican's behind-the-scenes efforts to save Jews during the Holocaust present a complex picture. While significant lives were saved through the actions of courageous clergy and religious orders, the limitations of these efforts highlight the moral dilemmas faced by the Church during one of history's darkest periods.

The Moral Complexity: Public Silence Versus Private Action

The juxtaposition of Pope Pius XII's public silence with the Vatican's private actions during the Holocaust creates a profound moral complexity. On one hand, the Church's efforts to shelter refugees and facilitate their escape demonstrate a commitment to humanitarian principles; on the other hand, the Pope's reluctance to publicly condemn the atrocities raises critical ethical questions about the role of religious leadership in times of crisis.

This complexity is further complicated by the notion of moral responsibility. As the spiritual leader of millions, Pope Pius XII held a unique position of influence. His words carried the potential to galvanize support for the Jewish community and inspire action against the Nazi regime. Critics argue that his failure to speak out publicly represented a betrayal of his moral duty, as silence in the face of genocide can be interpreted as complicity.

Conversely, defenders of Pius XII assert that public denunciation could have jeopardized the lives of countless Catholics and Jews. They contend that the Pope's calculated silence allowed for the preservation of the Church's influence and the continuation of its humanitarian efforts. In this view, Pius XII's actions, though discreet, were ultimately aimed at protecting lives rather than risking them through public condemnation.

The moral dilemma faced by the Vatican during the Holocaust thus reflects a broader tension between ethical convictions and pragmatic realities. This tension is particularly evident when considering the scale of the atrocities unfolding across Europe. The challenge of balancing public condemnation with the need for diplomacy raises difficult questions about the moral implications of silence.

In assessing the Vatican's role during this period, it is essential to consider the broader historical context. The rise of totalitarian regimes, the complexities of wartime diplomacy, and the moral challenges inherent in such circumstances all contributed to the decisions made by the Vatican. While the Church's actions may have saved lives, they also invite scrutiny and reflection on the nature of moral leadership.

The legacy of Pope Pius XII's response to the Holocaust continues to evoke passionate debate and reflection. It serves as a reminder of the complexities inherent in moral decision-making and the profound responsibilities held by spiritual leaders in times of crisis. The Vatican's actions during the Holocaust remain a critical case study in the interplay between faith, ethics, and the pursuit of justice.

Chapter 6: The Vatican's Neutrality – Balancing Both Sides

The Challenge of Maintaining Vatican Neutrality Amidst Total War

During World War II, the Vatican faced significant challenges in maintaining its neutrality in a global conflict characterized by total war. Pope Pius XII, who ascended to the papacy just before the war began, sought to position the Holy See as a moral authority capable of mediating between the warring nations. However, the complexities of the geopolitical landscape and the rising tide of totalitarianism complicated the Vatican's efforts to remain neutral.

At the outset of the war, the Vatican was keenly aware of the dangers of taking sides. Pope Pius XII aimed to protect the Church's interests and preserve its influence in a time of unprecedented violence. The Vatican's neutral position was rooted in a long tradition of diplomacy, wherein it sought to act as a mediator in international disputes. However, as the war intensified, the Vatican found itself navigating a treacherous path between competing ideologies and military powers.

The challenges of maintaining neutrality were particularly pronounced in Europe, where countries were quickly aligning themselves with either the Axis or Allied powers. The Vatican's diplomatic efforts necessitated engagement with both sides, which raised questions about its moral integrity. Critics contended that by failing to take a definitive stance against the aggressors, the Vatican risked appearing complicit in their actions. This perception of complicity was compounded by the fact that many Catholics were suffering under the regimes of Hitler and Mussolini.

Pope Pius XII's attempts to mediate between the belligerents often placed him in difficult positions. While he sought to advocate for peace and humanitarian relief, he was also keenly aware that public denunciations of the Axis powers could provoke retaliation against the Church and its followers. This delicate balancing act became increasingly fraught as the war progressed, and reports of atrocities began to surface.

Moreover, the Vatican's neutrality was challenged by the moral imperatives of the time. The sheer scale of suffering and the atrocities committed by the Nazis necessitated a response from moral leaders. The Vatican's decision to maintain neutrality, while intended to preserve the Church's position, often led to criticism and disappointment from those who expected a more active stance against tyranny.

In this context, the Vatican's neutrality was not merely a diplomatic strategy; it was also a moral dilemma. The Pope faced immense pressure to use his voice to speak out against the injustices unfolding across Europe. However, he believed that maintaining the Vatican's neutral position would ultimately enable the Church to fulfill its mission of humanitarian aid and support for the suffering.

As the war continued, the Vatican's neutrality remained a double-edged sword. While it allowed for the preservation of the Church's influence, it also led to increased scrutiny and criticism from various quarters. Many questioned whether the Vatican's actions aligned with its moral teachings and whether silence in the face of atrocity constituted a betrayal of its fundamental values.

How the Vatican Tried to Mediate Between Belligerents

Despite the challenges posed by maintaining neutrality, the Vatican actively sought to mediate between the belligerents during World War II. Pope Pius XII aimed to leverage the Holy See's unique position to foster dialogue and promote peace, often engaging in behind-the-scenes diplomacy in an attempt to mitigate the war's impact on civilians.

One of the key avenues through which the Vatican sought to mediate was through direct communication with both the Axis and Allied powers. Pius XII frequently dispatched letters to world leaders, urging

THE ROLE OF THE VATICAN IN WWII 37

them to pursue peaceful resolutions to their conflicts. These letters often included appeals for humanitarian efforts and calls to protect vulnerable populations, particularly those suffering under occupation.

The Vatican also used its diplomatic channels to communicate with neutral countries, hoping to act as an intermediary for negotiations. For instance, the Holy See maintained relations with Switzerland, which served as a hub for diplomatic discussions during the war. The Vatican worked to facilitate communication between belligerent nations, promoting dialogue and attempting to prevent further escalation of hostilities.

In addition to diplomatic communications, the Vatican's humanitarian efforts served as a platform for mediation. The Pope emphasized the need for compassion and assistance to war victims, regardless of their nationality. This focus on humanitarian action aligned with the Vatican's broader mission and provided an avenue for the Church to assert its moral authority amidst the chaos of war.

Pope Pius XII also sought to mediate through public statements, although these were often cautious and measured. In his Christmas message in 1942, for example, the Pope made veiled references to the suffering of innocents, which many interpreted as a subtle condemnation of the Holocaust. While these statements were intended to appeal to a sense of moral duty, they often lacked the explicitness that critics demanded.

The Vatican's efforts to mediate were not without their limitations. As the war dragged on, it became increasingly difficult to engage both sides in meaningful dialogue. The Axis powers, particularly Nazi Germany, became more entrenched in their ideology, making compromise challenging. The Vatican's attempts to mediate were often met with skepticism from Allied leaders, who questioned the sincerity of its neutrality.

Despite these challenges, the Vatican's mediatory efforts underscored its commitment to peace and humanitarian principles. The Pope's belief in the power of diplomacy and dialogue, even in the face of overwhelming violence, reflected a steadfast adherence to the Church's mission. However, the effectiveness of these efforts was ultimately limited by the realities of a world engulfed in total war.

The Criticism of Vatican Neutrality as Passive Complicity

The Vatican's decision to maintain neutrality during World War II has long been the subject of intense scrutiny and criticism. Many observers argue that the Vatican's silence and inaction in the face of the atrocities committed by the Axis powers amounted to passive complicity. This perception was particularly pronounced regarding the Holocaust, as the Vatican's reluctance to condemn the Nazis publicly led to widespread disillusionment among Jews and those fighting against fascism.

Critics of Vatican neutrality contend that the Church's failure to speak out against the actions of the Nazis reflected a profound moral failing. They argue that the Vatican, as a moral authority, had a responsibility to denounce the systematic extermination of Jews and other persecuted groups. By remaining silent, the Church is seen as having missed an opportunity to galvanize international opinion against the horrors of the Holocaust.

This criticism is compounded by the fact that many Catholic clergy and laypeople in occupied territories acted courageously to protect Jews and resist Nazi policies. While individual priests and nuns risked their lives to shelter refugees, the Vatican's central leadership appeared passive. This discrepancy between local action and Vatican policy raised questions about the moral integrity of the Church's leadership during a time of crisis.

Furthermore, the perception of passive complicity was exacerbated by the Vatican's diplomatic engagements with both Axis and Allied powers. Critics argued that the Vatican's attempts to maintain neutrality often translated into a reluctance to take a moral stand. By treating both sides equally, the Vatican risked diluting its moral authority and failing to support those fighting against tyranny.

Defenders of Vatican neutrality, however, argue that the complexities of wartime diplomacy necessitated a cautious approach. They contend that an outspoken denunciation of the Nazis could have led to severe repercussions for Catholics in occupied Europe, potentially endangering lives and diminishing the Church's ability to provide humanitarian assistance. In this view, the Pope's measured approach was intended to navigate the treacherous waters of total war while preserving the Church's mission.

Nonetheless, the criticism of Vatican neutrality persists, raising difficult ethical questions about the responsibilities of spiritual leaders during times of moral crisis. The expectation that the Church should serve as a beacon of hope and justice in the face of atrocity remains a central tenet of Catholic social teaching.

The debate surrounding Vatican neutrality during World War II continues to evoke strong emotions and differing interpretations. As historians and theologians grapple with the complexities of this period, the moral implications of silence, inaction, and diplomacy remain critical areas of exploration. Ultimately, the Vatican's neutrality serves as a case study in the challenges of moral leadership in a world marked by profound injustice and suffering.

Chapter 7: Vatican Involvement in Secret Peace Talks

The Vatican as a Mediator: Secret Talks with Both Axis and Allied Representatives

During World War II, the Vatican sought to position itself as a mediator in the conflict, believing that it could leverage its unique standing to facilitate peace negotiations. Pope Pius XII and other Vatican officials engaged in secret talks with both Axis and Allied representatives in an effort to advocate for diplomacy over warfare. This mediation was rooted in a deep commitment to the Church's mission of promoting peace and alleviating human suffering.

One of the primary avenues for the Vatican's diplomatic efforts was through its extensive network of contacts with various governments. Despite its official neutrality, the Vatican maintained relationships with key leaders in both Axis and Allied countries. This allowed the Holy See to serve as an intermediary, providing a platform for dialogue during a time when direct communication between belligerent nations was fraught with hostility and suspicion.

The Vatican's mediation efforts included discreet communications with Nazi Germany, Fascist Italy, and Allied powers such as the United States and the United Kingdom. Notably, Cardinal Eugenio Pacelli (later Pope Pius XII) played a crucial role in these negotiations. His understanding of international diplomacy and familiarity with political dynamics allowed the Vatican to engage with both sides effectively.

The Vatican's secret peace talks were often conducted through back channels, reflecting the sensitive nature of wartime diplomacy. This secrecy was essential in maintaining the confidence of both parties and ensuring that discussions could proceed without public scrutiny or political backlash. By positioning itself as a neutral entity, the Vatican aimed to foster an environment conducive to negotiations.

Several key moments in the war prompted Vatican involvement in peace talks. For example, as the war reached a stalemate in 1943, there were increasing calls for negotiations to end the fighting. The Vatican saw this as an opportunity to advocate for an armistice and to push for a ceasefire that could potentially lead to lasting peace. These efforts were met with cautious optimism by some leaders who recognized the Vatican's influence, but others were skeptical of the Church's motives.

Despite the Vatican's earnest attempts at mediation, the outcomes of these secret talks were often limited. Many leaders remained unconvinced that the Vatican could play a meaningful role in the negotiations, viewing it as overly cautious or even irrelevant in the face of the conflict's complexity. The Vatican's stance of neutrality was both an asset and a liability, making it difficult to gain the trust of either side.

Efforts to Broker Peace or Armistices During Pivotal Moments

The Vatican's efforts to broker peace and negotiate armistices during World War II were marked by a series of initiatives aimed at addressing the escalating violence and humanitarian crises resulting from the conflict. Pope Pius XII and his advisors recognized the urgent need for a diplomatic resolution to the war, and they sought to position the Vatican as a central player in these discussions.

One of the most significant moments for Vatican diplomacy occurred in 1943, when Allied forces began to make headway against Axis powers in North Africa. As the war shifted, the Vatican took the opportunity to promote peace talks between the belligerents. The Pope's Christmas address that year included an appeal for peace, urging nations to set aside their differences and seek reconciliation. This message resonated with some leaders who were contemplating a ceasefire, but it also drew criticism from others who felt that the Vatican's calls for peace were naive in light of the ongoing atrocities.

In addition to public appeals, the Vatican sought to engage in direct negotiations with key military and political leaders. The Holy See reached out to representatives from both sides, including intermediaries who could facilitate discussions. For instance, the Vatican explored the possibility of communicating with Italian officials who were disillusioned with Mussolini's regime, advocating for a shift towards peace negotiations.

Throughout these efforts, the Vatican also emphasized the importance of addressing the humanitarian crises resulting from the war. The Church's extensive charitable network allowed it to highlight the suffering of civilians caught in the crossfire, appealing to the moral sensibilities of leaders on both sides. By framing the discussion in terms of humanitarian need, the Vatican hoped to create a sense of urgency around the need for peace.

However, the Vatican's peace initiatives were often met with skepticism and reluctance. Leaders on both sides were grappling with their own strategic priorities, and many viewed negotiations as a sign of weakness. The complex realities of wartime politics—combined with competing national interests—made it difficult for the Vatican to gain traction in its peace efforts.

Furthermore, as the war progressed, divisions deepened between the Axis and Allied powers, complicating the Vatican's mediation role. The internal politics of both sides created an atmosphere of mistrust that hindered any potential for meaningful dialogue. This mistrust was particularly pronounced in the case of Nazi Germany, where the regime's totalitarian nature made any negotiation seem futile.

Ultimately, while the Vatican's peace initiatives reflected a genuine desire to promote diplomacy, they were often stymied by the harsh realities of wartime politics. The failure to secure an armistice during these pivotal moments underscored the challenges of diplomatic mediation in a world engulfed in conflict.

Why These Efforts Failed to Materialize: Conflicting Interests and Mistrust

Despite the Vatican's earnest attempts to mediate peace during World War II, the reality of conflicting interests and deep-seated mistrust ultimately undermined these efforts. The complexities of international relations during wartime created an environment where meaningful dialogue was fraught with challenges.

One of the primary reasons for the failure of Vatican peace initiatives was the divergent interests of the belligerent nations. Each side had its own strategic priorities, and the prospect of negotiating a ceasefire often seemed secondary to military objectives. For the Axis powers, maintaining territorial gains and asserting dominance took precedence over any consideration of peace talks. Similarly, Allied leaders were focused on defeating the Axis and were often unwilling to entertain discussions perceived as compromising their military efforts.

Additionally, the wartime climate was characterized by deep mistrust among the nations involved. The atrocities committed by the Axis powers, particularly the Holocaust, created a sense of moral outrage that colored perceptions of any diplomatic overtures. Allied leaders, especially, were hesitant to engage with representatives from regimes responsible for such widespread suffering. This mistrust extended to the Vatican itself, which some viewed as overly conciliatory toward the Axis.

The Vatican's neutral position, while intended to facilitate dialogue, also contributed to skepticism about its role in the peace process. Critics accused the Holy See of lacking the necessary moral clarity to take a definitive stance against tyranny. This perception hindered the Vatican's ability to act as a credible mediator, as leaders on both sides questioned its commitment to opposing Nazi aggression.

Moreover, the Vatican's diplomatic channels were often limited by the realities of wartime communication. The secrecy that surrounded negotiations made it difficult to build consensus and establish trust among the parties involved. This lack of transparency hampered the Vatican's ability to create a conducive environment for productive discussions.

In retrospect, the Vatican's involvement in secret peace talks during World War II serves as a poignant reminder of the complexities of wartime diplomacy. The challenges of conflicting interests, mistrust, and the moral imperatives of the time converged to thwart the Vatican's efforts to broker peace. Ultimately, these failed initiatives highlight the difficulties of navigating a landscape marked by profound violence and ethical dilemmas.

THE ROLE OF THE VATICAN IN WWII 45

Chapter 8: The Church's Role in Occupied Europe.

The Vatican's Communication with Catholic Clergy in Occupied Territories

Throughout World War II, the Vatican maintained communication with Catholic clergy in occupied territories, striving to provide guidance and support amid the challenges posed by totalitarian regimes. This communication was vital, as local clergy often found themselves in precarious situations, navigating the complexities of occupation while remaining faithful to their religious duties.

Pope Pius XII understood the critical role that local clergy could play in promoting resistance against oppression and safeguarding the rights of the faithful. As such, the Vatican established a system of communication to relay messages of support, encouragement, and guidance to bishops and priests in affected areas. These communications emphasized the importance of pastoral care and compassion, particularly in the face of persecution and violence.

In occupied countries like Poland, France, and the Netherlands, clergy faced immense pressure from occupying forces to conform to their demands. The Vatican encouraged priests to remain steadfast in their faith and to act as moral voices within their communities. These messages often stressed the necessity of helping those in need, including refugees and marginalized populations, regardless of their background or faith.

However, communication from the Vatican was often fraught with limitations. The realities of war made it challenging to relay messages consistently, and local clergy sometimes faced retaliation for their actions. In some instances, the Vatican's guidance could not be fully implemented due to the oppressive environments in which these priests operated. Nevertheless, the Vatican's outreach was crucial in bolstering the spirits of clergy who sought to navigate the difficult terrain of occupation.

Moreover, the Vatican's communication channels facilitated the exchange of information regarding the conditions of the faithful in occupied territories. Clergy reported back to the Vatican about the atrocities they witnessed, including the deportation of Jews and the persecution of political dissidents. These reports informed the Vatican's understanding of the dire humanitarian crisis unfolding across Europe and shaped its responses to the situation.

The Vatican's efforts to communicate with local clergy exemplified its commitment to maintaining a connection with the Church throughout Europe, despite the physical and ideological barriers imposed by occupation. The messages sent from Rome served not only as directives but also as expressions of solidarity with those suffering under totalitarian rule.

The Dilemmas Faced by Local Churches: Collaborating With, Resisting, or Surviving Occupation

Local churches in occupied Europe faced profound dilemmas during World War II, as they grappled with the realities of collaboration, resistance, and survival under oppressive regimes. The decisions made by clergy and congregations were often complex and deeply influenced by the political and social contexts in which they operated.

In some cases, local clergy found themselves collaborating with occupying forces in a bid to protect their congregations. This collaboration often stemmed from a desire to safeguard the Church's interests and maintain a semblance of normalcy in a time of chaos. For instance, some priests in France negotiated with German authorities to ensure the safety of their parishioners, seeking to balance the demands of the occupiers with their responsibilities to their communities. While these actions were sometimes motivated by a genuine desire to protect the faithful, they also drew criticism for appearing to condone the actions of the occupiers.

Conversely, many clergy chose to resist the oppressive measures imposed by the occupying forces. This resistance manifested in various forms, from providing sanctuary to persecuted individuals to actively participating in underground movements. In countries like Poland, priests played a crucial role in organizing resistance efforts, using their positions to rally support for anti-Nazi activities. These acts of defiance often came at great personal risk, as clergy faced severe repercussions for their actions, including imprisonment and execution.

The struggle for survival also influenced the choices made by local churches. Many clergy and congregations were forced to navigate the complexities of occupation while prioritizing their own safety. In some instances, churches were repurposed as shelters for refugees, providing essential support to those fleeing persecution. These actions exemplified the Church's commitment to humanitarian principles, even amidst the moral ambiguities of collaboration and resistance.

The dilemmas faced by local churches were further complicated by the theological and ethical considerations inherent in their decisions. Many clergy wrestled with the question of how to balance their spiritual responsibilities with the harsh realities of occupation. This internal conflict often led to profound moral dilemmas, as priests and bishops navigated the tension between faith and political realities.

Ultimately, the responses of local churches to occupation varied widely, influenced by the unique circumstances of each region. Some clergy chose collaboration as a means of survival, while others embraced resistance as a moral imperative. These choices reflected the complexities of navigating faith and politics in a time of profound moral crisis.

Notable Catholic Resistance Figures During the War: Priests and Bishops Aiding Jews and Dissidents

Amidst the turmoil of World War II, several notable Catholic resistance figures emerged, demonstrating remarkable courage in their efforts to aid Jews and political dissidents. These priests and bishops exemplified the commitment of the Church to humanitarian principles, often at great personal risk.

One of the most prominent figures was **Father Maximilian Kolbe**, a Polish Franciscan priest who became a symbol of self-sacrifice and compassion. After being arrested by the Gestapo for his anti-Nazi activities, Kolbe was sent to Auschwitz. There, he volunteered to take the place of a fellow prisoner condemned to death. His actions highlighted the moral courage of clergy willing to stand against tyranny and oppression. Kolbe's legacy would later be recognized when he was canonized as a saint by the Catholic Church.

In France, **Bishop Jules-Géraud Saliège** of Toulouse became an outspoken advocate for the rights of Jews. In 1942, he issued a pastoral letter condemning the deportation of Jews and calling for their protection. His bold stance resonated with many in the Catholic community and inspired numerous clergy and laypeople to take action against the injustices inflicted upon Jews. Saliège's efforts underscored the potential for the Church to act as a moral voice in the face of oppression.

Another notable figure was **Father Giovanni Battista Montini**, who would later become Pope Paul VI. During the war, Montini served as an official in the Vatican's Secretariat of State, where he played a pivotal role in coordinating humanitarian efforts to assist victims of Nazi persecution. His commitment to protecting the vulnerable and advocating for peace was evident in his work, which laid the groundwork for his future papacy.

In addition to these prominent figures, many lesser-known priests and religious orders also engaged in acts of resistance and humanitarian assistance. Some religious communities sheltered Jews, provided false identification papers, and facilitated escape routes to safety. These efforts often relied on the solidarity and bravery of local clergy, who risked their own safety to protect those targeted by the Nazis.

The contributions of these resistance figures serve as a testament to the potential for moral action within the Church, even in the darkest of times. Their commitment to aiding the persecuted and resisting oppression highlights the role of Catholic clergy as agents of change and compassion during World War II.

Chapter 9: Vatican Views on Communism and the Soviet Union

The Vatican's Strong Anti-Communist Stance During the War

During World War II, the Vatican adopted a strong anti-communist stance, viewing communism not only as a political ideology but also as a direct challenge to the teachings and authority of the Catholic Church. Pope Pius XII and his advisors were particularly alarmed by the spread of communism, especially following the Bolshevik Revolution in Russia in 1917, which had established a regime that explicitly rejected religious faith and sought to eradicate religious institutions.

The Vatican's opposition to communism intensified during the war, as the Church recognized the potential threat it posed to both religious freedom and social stability. The rise of communist movements in various parts of Europe, alongside the Soviet Union's military might, solidified the Vatican's resolve to combat what it perceived as a moral and existential threat.

This anti-communist sentiment was reflected in the Vatican's diplomatic communications and public statements. The Holy See issued various condemnations of communism, emphasizing its atheistic underpinnings and its inherent conflict with Christian values. The Vatican sought to rally support from other nations and religious communities against the spread of communism, positioning itself as a defender of Christian civilization in the face of totalitarian ideologies.

Moreover, the Vatican's anti-communist stance was not solely reactive; it was also proactive in seeking alliances with countries opposed to communist expansion. The Vatican engaged in diplomacy with nations that shared its concerns about the influence of the Soviet Union, including the United States and other Allied powers. This strategy aimed to bolster resistance against communism and promote the establishment of governments that would safeguard religious freedoms and human rights.

The Vatican's anti-communist rhetoric resonated with many Catholic communities across Europe, particularly in nations that were directly threatened by communist ideologies. The Church positioned itself as a moral authority, encouraging Catholics to stand firm against communism while advocating for democratic values and social justice. This rhetoric was particularly effective in mobilizing support within Eastern Europe, where the Church played a crucial role in resisting communist ideologies and advocating for human rights.

Ultimately, the Vatican's strong anti-communist stance during World War II was a defining characteristic of its foreign policy and diplomatic engagements. This position not only shaped the Church's actions during the war but also laid the groundwork for its post-war responses to the evolving geopolitical landscape.

How Anti-Communism Shaped Its Relations with Nazi Germany and Post-War Planning

The Vatican's anti-communist stance significantly influenced its relations with Nazi Germany, particularly as both regimes shared a mutual disdain for communism. While the Vatican maintained its official neutrality during the war, its position on communism affected its diplomatic strategies and interactions with the Axis powers.

Initially, the Vatican viewed the rise of the Nazi regime as a potential bulwark against the spread of communism. Pope Pius XI, before his death in 1939, expressed concerns about the dangers of Bolshevism, and this perspective carried over to Pius XII's papacy. The Vatican sought to negotiate with Nazi Germany to protect the rights of the Church and to ensure that religious freedoms would not be compromised. This pragmatic approach reflected a calculated effort to navigate the complexities of a rapidly changing political landscape.

However, as the true nature of the Nazi regime became evident, particularly with its oppressive measures against the Church and its horrific policies towards Jews and other marginalized groups, the Vatican faced a moral dilemma. While it had initially hoped to establish a working relationship with Germany, the escalating atrocities forced the Church to reconsider its stance. The Vatican issued statements condemning the persecution of Jews and advocating for humanitarian concerns, although these actions were often criticized for lacking sufficient forcefulness.

In the aftermath of World War II, the Vatican's anti-communist ideology heavily influenced its post-war planning and its responses to the geopolitical shifts in Europe. The rise of the Soviet Union as a superpower and the subsequent spread of communism in Eastern Europe raised alarms within the Church. The Vatican recognized the potential for communist ideologies to undermine religious freedoms and threaten the Catholic Church's influence in these regions.

As the Cold War began to take shape, the Vatican became increasingly engaged in diplomatic efforts to counter Soviet expansion. The Church sought to support Catholic communities in Eastern Europe, particularly in countries like Poland, Hungary, and Czechoslovakia, where communist regimes posed significant challenges to religious practice. The Vatican provided financial and logistical support to these communities, aiming to empower them in their resistance against oppressive governments.

The Vatican's anti-communist stance also played a role in shaping its relationships with Western powers. As the United States and its allies adopted containment strategies against communism, the Vatican positioned itself as a moral ally in these efforts. This alignment facilitated collaboration between the Vatican and Western governments, with the Church advocating for policies that promoted religious freedoms and democratic values.

Ultimately, the Vatican's anti-communism served as a guiding principle in its relations with Nazi Germany during the war and its subsequent post-war planning. The Church's focus on countering communism informed its diplomatic strategies and shaped its interactions with both Axis and Allied powers, influencing the course of European politics in the aftermath of the conflict.

Post-War Concerns About Soviet Expansion into Eastern Europe and the Fate of Catholic Communities

As World War II drew to a close, the Vatican faced significant concerns regarding the expansion of Soviet influence into Eastern Europe. The establishment of communist regimes in several countries raised alarms within the Catholic Church, which recognized the potential threat to religious freedoms and the survival of Catholic communities in the region.

The Vatican closely monitored the developments in Eastern Europe, particularly in countries like Poland, Hungary, and Czechoslovakia, where the Church had a long-standing presence. The imposition of communist rule often led to the suppression of religious practices, the persecution of clergy, and the closure of churches. The Vatican viewed these actions as a direct assault on the rights of Catholics and an affront to the Church's mission.

In response to these concerns, the Vatican sought to protect Catholic communities and support their resilience against oppressive regimes. The Church established communication channels with local bishops and clergy in Eastern Europe, providing them with guidance and encouragement as they navigated the challenges of living under communist rule. The Vatican emphasized the importance of maintaining faith and solidarity among Catholics, urging local leaders to resist pressures to conform to the state.

Additionally, the Vatican engaged in diplomatic efforts to advocate for the rights of Catholics in Eastern Europe. Through its diplomatic representatives and networks, the Holy See sought to raise awareness of the plight of Catholic communities and to garner support from Western powers. The Vatican emphasized the need for religious freedoms to be included in post-war agreements, advocating for the protection of minority rights in newly established communist states.

Despite these efforts, the Vatican faced significant limitations in its ability to effect change. The political realities of the post-war landscape, coupled with the Soviet Union's assertive stance, made it difficult for the Church to exert meaningful influence. In many instances, local clergy and Catholic communities were left to navigate their struggles largely without external support.

The Vatican's concerns about Soviet expansion and its implications for Catholic communities laid the groundwork for its engagement in the Cold War. The Church positioned itself as a defender of religious freedom and human rights, emphasizing the importance of faith in the face of totalitarianism. This advocacy resonated with many Catholics worldwide and helped to galvanize support for those suffering under oppressive regimes.

In summary, the post-war expansion of Soviet influence in Eastern Europe presented significant challenges for the Vatican and Catholic communities. The Church's efforts to protect these communities reflected its commitment to preserving faith and dignity in the face of political oppression, as well as its broader mission to advocate for religious freedoms globally.

Chapter 10: Vatican Assistance to War Refugees

The Vatican's Efforts to Assist Refugees Fleeing the War

During World War II, the Vatican took significant measures to assist the millions of refugees fleeing conflict and persecution across Europe. As the war escalated and the humanitarian crisis deepened, the Vatican recognized its moral obligation to provide support to those displaced by violence and oppression.

Pope Pius XII made it clear that the Church had a duty to act in defense of human dignity and to alleviate the suffering of refugees. The Vatican established a network of contacts and communication channels to identify and assist those in need, emphasizing compassion and humanitarianism as central tenets of its mission. This effort included offering shelter, food, and medical assistance to refugees seeking safety from the chaos of war.

The Holy See also sought to leverage its diplomatic relations to facilitate aid efforts. Vatican officials engaged with various governments and international organizations, advocating for the protection of refugees and urging nations to open their borders to those fleeing persecution. The Church's unique position allowed it to navigate the complexities of international politics, highlighting the plight of refugees in negotiations and discussions with both Axis and Allied powers.

One notable aspect of the Vatican's refugee assistance was its commitment to helping Jewish refugees. As the Holocaust unfolded and Jews faced systematic extermination, the Vatican worked discreetly to provide sanctuary for those fleeing Nazi persecution. This included arranging for the issuance of false identity papers, sheltering refugees in convents and monasteries, and coordinating with local clergy to ensure safe passage to more secure areas. While the extent of these efforts remains a subject of historical debate, there is evidence that individual clergy and religious orders took significant risks to protect Jews and other vulnerable groups during this dark period.

The Vatican's actions reflected a broader commitment to humanitarian principles, demonstrating that the Church sought not only to protect its interests but also to embody the teachings of Christ in its response to suffering. The assistance provided by the Vatican and local Church organizations was often a lifeline for refugees, offering hope amid despair and uncertainty.

Collaboration with Catholic Humanitarian Organizations

To maximize its impact and reach in assisting war refugees, the Vatican collaborated closely with various Catholic humanitarian organizations. These organizations, both established and newly formed during the war, played a crucial role in delivering aid and support to those in need.

One of the prominent organizations was the **International Catholic Migration Commission (ICMC)**, established in 1951 but with roots tracing back to the post-war period. The Vatican played a vital role in fostering cooperation among different Catholic charities and organizations dedicated to humanitarian assistance. Through these partnerships, the Church was able to coordinate efforts and pool resources, ensuring a more efficient and effective response to the refugee crisis.

In addition to the ICMC, other Catholic relief organizations, such as **Caritas Internationalis**, mobilized to provide support to refugees. Caritas, with its extensive network of local branches across Europe, facilitated the delivery of essential services, including food distribution, medical care, and shelter. The collaboration between the Vatican and these organizations enabled a swift and organized response to the needs of displaced individuals and families.

The Vatican also worked with non-Catholic humanitarian groups and international agencies, recognizing the importance of solidarity across faith lines in addressing the humanitarian crisis. This collaboration allowed for the sharing of information, resources, and strategies to assist refugees effectively. By fostering a spirit of cooperation among various organizations, the Vatican aimed to create a more comprehensive and compassionate response to the needs of those affected by war.

Through these partnerships, the Vatican was able to amplify its humanitarian efforts, reaching more individuals and communities in need. The collaboration with Catholic and non-Catholic organizations highlighted the Church's commitment to working towards the common good, transcending denominational boundaries in the face of human suffering.

How Vatican Diplomacy Facilitated Aid Delivery to Occupied or War-Torn Regions

The Vatican's diplomatic efforts played a critical role in facilitating aid delivery to occupied or war-torn regions during World War II. Leveraging its unique position as a neutral entity, the Vatican engaged with various governments, international organizations, and local authorities to negotiate access for humanitarian assistance in areas most affected by conflict.

Pope Pius XII and his advisors used diplomacy to advocate for the rights of refugees and the need for humanitarian aid. The Vatican communicated directly with both Axis and Allied powers, emphasizing the moral obligation to protect vulnerable populations. These diplomatic overtures often included appeals to national leaders, urging them to allow for the safe passage of aid and to prioritize the needs of civilians in occupied territories.

In particular, the Vatican sought to address the needs of refugees in regions where access was severely restricted. The Church's representatives engaged with local authorities and military commanders, negotiating arrangements to ensure that aid could reach those in need. These efforts were often met with challenges, as wartime politics and military strategies complicated the logistics of delivering assistance. Nevertheless, the Vatican's diplomatic channels provided a platform for advocating for humanitarian needs amid the chaos of war.

One notable example of the Vatican's diplomatic efforts involved negotiations regarding the plight of Jews in occupied Europe. As Nazi Germany implemented its genocidal policies, the Vatican worked to secure protections for Jewish communities and to facilitate escape routes for those at risk. Through its diplomatic representatives, the Vatican engaged with both local and foreign officials to advocate for the safe passage of Jewish refugees, emphasizing the moral imperative to protect innocent lives.

The Vatican's diplomacy also extended to post-war planning, as officials sought to address the long-term needs of war-torn regions. The Holy See actively participated in discussions regarding the reconstruction of Europe and the reintegration of displaced individuals into society. This involved advocating for policies that would promote social justice, religious freedom, and the protection of human rights in the aftermath of the war.

In summary, the Vatican's diplomacy was instrumental in facilitating aid delivery to occupied or war-torn regions during World War II. Through its engagement with various stakeholders, the Vatican sought to address the urgent humanitarian needs of refugees and to advocate for the rights and dignity of those affected by conflict. The Church's commitment to humanitarian principles underscored its broader mission to promote peace and justice in a world ravaged by war.

Chapter 11: Controversies Surrounding Pope Pius XII's Silence

The Accusation of "Silent Complicity" with Nazi Atrocities

Pope Pius XII's leadership during World War II has been a focal point of intense scrutiny and controversy, particularly regarding his perceived silence on the atrocities committed by the Nazi regime. Critics have accused him of "silent complicity," suggesting that his failure to vocally condemn the Holocaust and other acts of persecution indicated an unwillingness to confront evil. This view posits that the Pope's silence allowed the Nazi regime to continue its genocidal policies unchecked, as he seemingly prioritized diplomatic relations and the Church's neutrality over moral advocacy.

The accusation of silent complicity stems from several key moments during the war when Pius XII could have used his position to speak out against the atrocities. For instance, in 1942, reports of mass exterminations were reaching the Vatican, yet Pius XII chose not to publicly denounce these actions in a manner that many deemed appropriate. Instead, he focused on maintaining diplomatic relations with Germany and other Axis powers, a strategy some argue was necessary to protect the Church and its interests.

Critics also highlight that Pius XII had opportunities to intervene more forcefully on behalf of Jews and other persecuted groups. Many believe that his silence was not merely a diplomatic strategy but rather a moral failing, as it contradicted the Church's teachings on the sanctity of human life and the duty to protect the vulnerable. The notion that the Vatican could have played a more active role in advocating for Jewish lives has been a source of deep frustration for historians, theologians, and Jewish communities alike.

The weight of this accusation has not only affected Pius XII's legacy but has also had broader implications for the Catholic Church. The perception that the Pope failed to act against one of history's most heinous crimes has led to long-lasting questions about the Church's moral authority and its role in advocating for justice during times of crisis.

This controversy surrounding Pius XII's silence continues to resonate today, sparking ongoing debates about the responsibilities of religious leaders in times of war, the complexities of moral decision-making, and the lasting consequences of inaction in the face of evil.

Defenses of Pope Pius XII's Actions: Contextualizing His Cautious Diplomacy

In response to the accusations of silent complicity, defenders of Pope Pius XII argue that his actions must be understood within the complex political and social context of World War II. They contend that his cautious diplomacy was a necessary strategy aimed at protecting the Catholic Church and its followers during a time of unprecedented peril.

Supporters point out that the Vatican's primary goal was to maintain its sovereignty and the safety of Catholics in Europe. Pius XII's approach was influenced by the fear of further persecution, particularly after the devastating effects of previous anti-Catholic measures taken by totalitarian regimes in Europe. Given the oppressive environment, it was imperative for the Pope to navigate carefully to ensure that the Church could continue its work, including humanitarian efforts, amidst the turmoil.

Moreover, proponents of Pius XII highlight his behind-the-scenes actions, which included diplomatic efforts to protect Jews and other marginalized groups. While he may not have made public declarations against the Nazis, it is argued that he worked discreetly to save lives.

Instances of the Vatican providing shelter, issuing false identity papers, and facilitating the escape of Jews are cited as evidence of Pius XII's commitment to humanitarianism, even if those actions did not receive widespread public acknowledgment.

Defenders also assert that the nature of Vatican diplomacy during the war was inherently complex. The Pope faced significant challenges in communicating effectively with both Axis and Allied powers. Public denunciations of Nazi atrocities could have jeopardized the Vatican's ability to negotiate and mediate in the crisis, potentially exacerbating the suffering of those he aimed to protect. This argument posits that a more vocal opposition could have led to severe reprisals against Catholics and other groups in Nazi-occupied territories.

Furthermore, some historians emphasize the challenges of the time, noting that the full extent of the Holocaust was not widely known or understood, even among political leaders and religious figures. Pius XII was confronted with the grim reality of war, where information was often fragmented and uncertain. This context raises questions about the expectations placed on the Pope and the complexity of making moral decisions in such dire circumstances.

In summary, while criticisms of Pope Pius XII's silence remain prevalent, defenders of his actions argue that his cautious diplomacy was a calculated response to an extraordinarily complex situation. They contend that his behind-the-scenes efforts to save lives and protect the Church should be recognized alongside the critiques of his public stance during the war.

The Long-Term Impact on the Church's Reputation and Historical Memory

The controversies surrounding Pope Pius XII's actions during World War II have had lasting effects on the Catholic Church's reputation and historical memory. The accusations of silent complicity and moral failure have contributed to a polarized narrative that continues to shape public perceptions of the Church's role during one of history's darkest periods.

In the years following the war, the Church faced significant challenges in reconciling its actions during this time with the growing demand for accountability and transparency. The question of Pius XII's legacy became a prominent topic of discussion among theologians, historians, and the broader Catholic community. This scrutiny has led to a re-examination of the Church's moral authority and its commitment to social justice.

One of the most significant long-term impacts has been the erosion of trust among some segments of the Jewish community. Many Jews feel that the Vatican's actions during the Holocaust did not adequately reflect a commitment to the protection of their lives. This sentiment has fueled ongoing dialogue and sometimes tension between the Catholic Church and Jewish communities, complicating interfaith relations.

The controversy surrounding Pius XII has also influenced the Church's approach to its historical narrative. In recent years, the Vatican has made efforts to address the historical memory of World War II, engaging in dialogue with scholars and communities affected by the war. Initiatives to publish archives and promote research on this period reflect a desire for greater transparency and a willingness to confront difficult questions about the Church's past.

Furthermore, the debates surrounding Pius XII's legacy have prompted the Catholic Church to reevaluate its moral teachings and responsibilities in the face of injustice. The experience of World War II and the Holocaust have become integral to discussions on human rights, religious freedom, and the moral imperative to speak out against oppression. This re-examination has led to a renewed commitment to social justice, human dignity, and the protection of vulnerable populations in contemporary Church teaching.

In conclusion, the controversies surrounding Pope Pius XII's silence during World War II have left an indelible mark on the Catholic

Church's reputation and historical memory. The ongoing dialogue and reflection on this period continue to shape the Church's identity and its approach to moral and ethical challenges in the modern world.

Chapter 12: The Vatican's Post-War Role

The Vatican's Role in Post-War Reconciliation and the Rebuilding of Europe

In the aftermath of World War II, the Vatican emerged as a significant player in the efforts to reconcile nations and rebuild a war-torn Europe. Recognizing the urgent need for peace and stability, Pope Pius XII and his advisors sought to promote reconciliation among the nations that had been embroiled in conflict. The Vatican aimed to foster dialogue, understanding, and cooperation in a divided continent struggling to heal from the scars of war.

One of the Vatican's primary contributions to post-war reconciliation was its involvement in international organizations aimed at fostering peace. The Vatican supported initiatives such as the **United Nations** and the **European Community**, which were established to promote cooperation among nations and prevent future conflicts. By advocating for multilateral diplomacy and international collaboration, the Vatican sought to play a constructive role in shaping a new order based on mutual respect and understanding.

The Holy See also emphasized the importance of forgiveness and reconciliation as central tenets of its moral teaching. Pope Pius XII called for a spirit of charity and compassion among nations, urging leaders to prioritize the common good over nationalistic ambitions. This call for unity resonated strongly in a Europe that was still grappling with the repercussions of war and the ideological divides that had emerged.

In addition to promoting reconciliation among nations, the Vatican was deeply engaged in humanitarian efforts to assist those affected by the war. The Church mobilized resources to provide aid to countries devastated by conflict, focusing on rebuilding infrastructure, providing food and medical assistance, and addressing the needs of displaced

THE ROLE OF THE VATICAN IN WWII 65

populations. Through its extensive network of dioceses and charitable organizations, the Vatican aimed to alleviate the suffering of those who had endured the hardships of war.

Moreover, the Vatican's diplomatic efforts extended to fostering relationships with both Western and Eastern European nations. As the Cold War began to take shape, the Vatican sought to maintain its neutrality while advocating for dialogue between opposing ideologies. The Pope's diplomatic engagements aimed to bridge the divide between the capitalist West and the communist East, emphasizing the importance of dialogue in achieving lasting peace.

In summary, the Vatican played a vital role in post-war reconciliation and the rebuilding of Europe by promoting dialogue, fostering cooperation, and emphasizing humanitarian assistance. Its efforts aimed to create a more stable and peaceful Europe, rooted in the principles of justice and compassion.

Assisting Displaced Persons, Including Efforts to Reunite Families

As Europe emerged from the devastation of World War II, millions of people were left displaced, separated from their homes and families. The Vatican recognized the urgent need to assist these individuals and played a crucial role in efforts to support displaced persons (DPs) and facilitate family reunification.

The Vatican collaborated with various international organizations, including the **International Refugee Organization (IRO)**, to address the challenges faced by displaced populations. Through these partnerships, the Vatican aimed to provide essential services such as shelter, food, and medical care to those who had lost everything during the war. The Holy See's involvement in humanitarian efforts underscored its commitment to protecting human dignity and addressing the needs of the most vulnerable.

One of the significant focuses of the Vatican's efforts was the reunification of families torn apart by the war. Many individuals had been separated due to forced migrations, deportations, and the chaos of conflict. The Vatican worked to create pathways for family members to reconnect, recognizing the emotional and psychological toll of separation. The Church mobilized its resources to help locate missing persons and facilitate their return to their families.

Local dioceses and Catholic charities were instrumental in these efforts, utilizing their networks to track down displaced individuals and provide them with the necessary assistance to return home. This work involved collaboration with governmental agencies, non-governmental organizations, and other faith-based groups dedicated to addressing the needs of displaced populations.

In addition to practical support, the Vatican emphasized the importance of spiritual and emotional healing for displaced persons. Pope Pius XII recognized that the trauma of war extended beyond physical suffering and called for pastoral care to address the psychological and spiritual needs of those affected. The Church organized counseling services, support groups, and religious ceremonies to help individuals process their experiences and rebuild their lives.

Through its humanitarian initiatives, the Vatican aimed to restore hope and dignity to displaced persons, fostering a sense of community and belonging in a post-war world. The Church's commitment to assisting displaced individuals and facilitating family reunification was an integral part of its broader mission to promote peace and reconciliation in a fractured Europe.

Vatican Influence on Post-War Political Alliances: Support for Christian Democratic Movements in Europe

In the post-war period, the Vatican became increasingly involved in shaping political alliances in Europe, particularly through its support for

Christian Democratic movements. Recognizing the rise of communism as a significant threat to Christian values and social order, the Vatican sought to promote a political framework grounded in Catholic social teaching and democratic principles.

Christian Democracy emerged as a political force in several European countries after the war, advocating for a balanced approach that combined social justice with economic growth. The Vatican provided moral support to these movements, emphasizing the importance of a political system that upheld human dignity and promoted the common good. The Church's endorsement of Christian Democratic parties reflected its desire to counter the influence of communism and advocate for a society rooted in Christian values.

The Vatican's support for Christian Democratic movements was particularly evident in countries such as Italy, Germany, and France, where the Church had strong historical ties. In Italy, the **Christian Democracy Party** became a dominant political force in the post-war era, and the Vatican's backing was instrumental in its electoral successes. Similarly, in Germany, the **Christian Democratic Union (CDU)** emerged as a key player in shaping the country's post-war political landscape, with the Vatican's support reinforcing its legitimacy.

The Church's involvement in politics during this period was not without controversy. Critics argued that the Vatican's engagement in political affairs blurred the lines between church and state, raising questions about the appropriateness of religious influence on governance. Nevertheless, the Vatican maintained that its support for Christian Democratic movements was rooted in a commitment to social justice and the protection of human rights.

Moreover, the Vatican's influence extended beyond national politics to the broader European integration movement. The Holy See was an advocate for a united Europe based on shared values and principles, believing that cooperation among nations was essential for peace and stability. This vision aligned with the goals of Christian Democratic leaders who sought to promote European unity as a counterweight to the ideological divisions of the Cold War.

In conclusion, the Vatican's influence on post-war political alliances, particularly its support for Christian Democratic movements, reflected its commitment to promoting democratic values, social justice, and a united Europe. This engagement played a significant role in shaping the political landscape of post-war Europe and underscored the Church's ongoing mission to contribute to the common good in a changing world.

Chapter 13: The Vatican and Nazi War Criminals – The Ratlines

The Vatican's Involvement in Aiding War Criminals Escape to South America

In the immediate aftermath of World War II, the plight of Nazi war criminals became a pressing issue for many nations seeking justice for the atrocities committed during the Holocaust. However, a covert network known as the "Ratlines" emerged, facilitating the escape of numerous Nazis from Europe to South America, with the Vatican allegedly playing a significant role in this clandestine operation.

The term "Ratlines" refers to the various escape routes used by Nazi officials and collaborators to flee Europe. These networks often involved sympathetic clergy, including some in the Catholic Church, who provided logistical support, documentation, and safe passage to those fleeing prosecution. Reports suggest that several high-ranking Church officials were aware of, and in some cases actively participated in, these efforts.

One of the most notable figures associated with the Ratlines was **Archbishop Alois Hudal**, the Austrian priest and rector of the Pontifical Institute for the Foreign Missions in Rome. Hudal was known for his connections with Nazi officials and his willingness to aid their escape. He provided false identities and travel documents to individuals sought by Allied forces, helping them reach safe havens in countries like Argentina, Brazil, and Paraguay.

While the Vatican has consistently denied any official involvement in these operations, the Church's networks and resources facilitated the movement of numerous war criminals. The motives behind this assistance are complex and multifaceted, reflecting a combination of humanitarian concerns, political calculations, and, in some cases, ideological sympathies.

As a result of the Vatican's involvement, some notorious war criminals, including **Adolf Eichmann**, who played a pivotal role in organizing the logistics of the Holocaust, managed to escape capture. The ramifications of these actions have had lasting implications for both the Vatican and its relationship with international justice efforts.

The Vatican's complicity in aiding the escape of Nazi war criminals raised profound ethical questions about the Church's role in protecting individuals responsible for heinous crimes. This chapter aims to explore the various dimensions of the Ratlines, examining how they operated, the motivations behind the Vatican's actions, and the moral implications of providing refuge to war criminals.

How Vatican Figures Justified Their Actions

The actions of Vatican officials involved in the Ratlines were often justified through various rationalizations rooted in a complex interplay of moral, political, and theological considerations. Some Church leaders maintained that their involvement in aiding former Nazis was a matter of mercy, prioritizing compassion over retribution.

One of the primary justifications offered was the belief that the Church had a moral obligation to provide refuge to those fleeing persecution, regardless of their past actions. This perspective held that, in the spirit of Christian forgiveness, the Church should extend compassion to all, including those who had committed grave injustices. The idea was that by providing sanctuary, the Church could facilitate redemption and healing, even for those who had been part of the Nazi regime.

Moreover, some Vatican officials viewed the geopolitical landscape of post-war Europe as a reason to support former Nazis. In the context of the emerging Cold War, there was concern that communism could spread throughout Europe and Latin America. By assisting certain former Nazis, particularly those who were anti-communist, the Vatican aimed to counter the influence of communist movements and maintain a balance of power favorable to Western interests.

Additionally, there was a pragmatic element to these justifications. The Vatican recognized the value of certain individuals who had been part of the Nazi regime for their knowledge and connections. Some Church officials believed that these figures could serve as valuable allies in rebuilding Europe and opposing communism, thus viewing their assistance as a strategic necessity.

Despite these justifications, the actions of those involved in the Ratlines remain highly controversial. Critics argue that such rationalizations fail to account for the moral responsibility of the Church to confront evil and seek justice for the victims of the Holocaust. The legacy of these decisions has prompted ongoing debates about the ethical implications of the Church's actions during this tumultuous period.

In essence, the justifications provided by Vatican figures for aiding Nazi war criminals reflect a complex mixture of compassion, political strategy, and pragmatic considerations. However, these rationalizations have not diminished the moral weight of the Church's involvement in facilitating the escape of individuals responsible for some of history's most horrific atrocities.

The Long-Term Consequences for the Church's Image and Relations with Post-War Governments

The Vatican's involvement in the Ratlines and its assistance to Nazi war criminals has had profound and lasting consequences for the Church's image and its relationships with post-war governments. The revelations of the Vatican's complicity in aiding the escape of war criminals led to significant public outrage and scrutiny, damaging the Church's moral authority and credibility.

In the years following the war, investigations into the Ratlines exposed the extent of the Vatican's involvement, prompting widespread criticism from various sectors, including Jewish organizations, human rights advocates, and even within the Catholic community. Many viewed the Church's actions as a betrayal of its moral teachings and an affront to the victims of the Holocaust. The perception of the Vatican as a protector of war criminals undermined its efforts to position itself as a moral authority in post-war Europe.

Furthermore, the Church's reputation was further complicated by the evolving political landscape of the Cold War. As tensions escalated between the West and the Soviet Union, the Vatican found itself navigating a precarious relationship with governments that were increasingly critical of its past actions. While some Western governments initially sought to collaborate with the Vatican against communism, the revelation of its ties to former Nazis led to distrust and skepticism.

In response to these challenges, the Vatican has made efforts to address its legacy regarding the Ratlines. The Church has engaged in dialogue with Jewish communities and sought to clarify its position on issues related to the Holocaust. Various popes have publicly acknowledged the suffering of Holocaust victims and expressed remorse for the actions of individuals associated with the Church during that time.

Nevertheless, the shadow of the Ratlines continues to affect the Vatican's image and its relationships with post-war governments. The Church must grapple with the ethical implications of its past while striving to maintain its relevance in a changing world. The legacy of the Ratlines serves as a reminder of the complexities of moral decision-making in times of crisis and the enduring impact of historical actions on contemporary institutions.

In conclusion, the involvement of the Vatican in the Ratlines has left a lasting mark on the Church's image and its relations with post-war governments. The repercussions of these actions continue to reverberate, shaping the Church's efforts to address its past and navigate the moral complexities of the present.

Chapter 14: Legacy of the Vatican's WWII Diplomacy

The Impact of Vatican Diplomacy on Modern Church-State Relations

The Vatican's diplomacy during World War II has had a profound and lasting impact on modern Church-state relations, shaping how the Catholic Church engages with political entities and influences global affairs. The complexities of the Vatican's actions during the war have led to a reevaluation of its role in international politics, prompting both criticism and adaptation in its diplomatic strategies.

One of the most significant effects of Vatican diplomacy during WWII has been the increased scrutiny of the Church's involvement in political matters. The controversies surrounding Pope Pius XII's actions and the Vatican's alleged complicity in aiding Nazi war criminals have led to calls for greater transparency and accountability in the Church's dealings with state authorities. This heightened awareness has prompted the Vatican to adopt a more cautious approach to diplomacy, emphasizing the need for moral integrity and ethical considerations in its interactions with governments.

In response to the lessons learned from WWII, the Vatican has sought to reinforce the principle of human rights as a cornerstone of its diplomatic efforts. The Church has increasingly positioned itself as an advocate for social justice and the dignity of all individuals, aligning its diplomatic initiatives with contemporary human rights concerns. This shift reflects a commitment to address the moral implications of political actions, emphasizing the Church's role as a defender of the vulnerable and marginalized.

Moreover, the legacy of Vatican diplomacy during the war has influenced its relations with secular governments. The Church has recognized the importance of establishing constructive dialogues with state authorities, fostering partnerships that prioritize humanitarian efforts and conflict resolution. By engaging with governments on shared values, the Vatican aims to enhance its relevance in a global landscape marked by political polarization and social unrest.

Additionally, the challenges of maintaining neutrality during WWII have prompted the Vatican to reevaluate its stance on international conflicts. The Church has increasingly embraced a proactive role in promoting peace and reconciliation, advocating for dialogue as a means of resolving disputes. This approach reflects an understanding that the Church's moral authority can contribute to conflict resolution and peacebuilding efforts, positioning the Vatican as a mediator in contemporary global challenges.

In summary, the impact of Vatican diplomacy during World War II has reshaped modern Church-state relations by fostering a commitment to human rights, transparency, and ethical considerations in diplomatic engagements. The Church's evolving role in the political arena reflects its desire to uphold moral integrity while addressing contemporary global issues.

How Vatican Responses During WWII Have Shaped the Church's Modern Approach to Human Rights and Conflict

The responses of the Vatican during World War II have profoundly shaped the Church's modern approach to human rights and conflict resolution. The moral complexities and ethical dilemmas faced by Church leaders during the war have influenced the development of contemporary Church teachings on social justice, peace, and the dignity of human life.

One of the most significant impacts of the Vatican's responses during the war has been the elevation of human rights as a central concern in its diplomatic agenda. The atrocities committed during the Holocaust and the experiences of victims have prompted the Church to adopt a more proactive stance in advocating for the protection of human rights globally. This evolution is reflected in various papal encyclicals and documents that emphasize the dignity of every person and the importance of social justice as fundamental tenets of Catholic teaching.

Moreover, the Vatican's experiences during the war have underscored the necessity of addressing the root causes of conflict. The Church has recognized that wars are often driven by social, economic, and political injustices, and thus has sought to promote equitable solutions that address these underlying issues. This focus on justice and reconciliation aligns with the Church's commitment to peacebuilding, advocating for dialogue as a means of resolving disputes and fostering understanding among diverse communities.

The Vatican has also taken a more active role in international humanitarian efforts, seeking to provide assistance to those affected by conflict and violence. By collaborating with various organizations and agencies, the Church has positioned itself as a key player in addressing humanitarian crises, reflecting its commitment to upholding human dignity in the face of adversity.

Additionally, the Vatican has increasingly engaged with global institutions such as the United Nations, advocating for the implementation of human rights standards and the promotion of peace. This engagement demonstrates the Church's recognition of the interconnectedness of global issues and its responsibility to contribute to solutions that prioritize human rights and social justice.

In conclusion, the Vatican's responses during World War II have profoundly shaped its modern approach to human rights and conflict resolution. The Church's commitment to advocating for social justice, addressing the root causes of conflict, and engaging in humanitarian efforts reflects a desire to learn from the past and contribute positively to contemporary global challenges.

The Ongoing Debates Around Pope Pius XII's Canonization and the

THE ROLE OF THE VATICAN IN WWII

Release of Vatican WWII Archives

The legacy of Pope Pius XII and the Vatican's actions during World War II continue to spark significant debates, particularly regarding the canonization of Pius XII and the release of Vatican WWII archives. These discussions have profound implications for the Church's historical narrative and its relationship with Jewish communities and human rights advocates.

The canonization of Pope Pius XII has been a contentious issue, with strong opinions on both sides. Proponents argue that Pius XII acted with prudence and moral integrity during a tumultuous period, emphasizing his efforts to protect Jews and assist those fleeing persecution. They contend that his actions should be viewed within the context of the difficult decisions faced by leaders during wartime and that his canonization would recognize his commitment to the Church and the protection of human rights.

Conversely, critics argue that Pius XII's perceived silence on the Holocaust and the actions of the Vatican during the war raise serious ethical questions. Many Jewish organizations and historians contend that his inaction in publicly condemning the atrocities committed against Jews undermines any arguments for his canonization. The debates surrounding Pius XII's legacy highlight the ongoing struggles to confront the moral complexities of the Church's past and its role in addressing historical injustices.

The release of Vatican WWII archives has been another focal point of discussion in this context. Many scholars, journalists, and advocates have called for greater transparency regarding the Church's actions during the war, believing that access to archival materials could shed light on the Vatican's responses to the Holocaust and its diplomatic engagements. The Vatican has gradually begun to release some of these archives, allowing researchers to explore the complexities of the Church's involvement in wartime diplomacy.

The careful examination of these archives may provide a more nuanced understanding of the Vatican's role during WWII, offering insights into the motivations and decisions of Church leaders. However, the process has been slow, and many advocates argue that a full and transparent disclosure is necessary to rebuild trust with affected communities and ensure accountability for past actions.

In summary, the ongoing debates surrounding Pope Pius XII's canonization and the release of Vatican WWII archives reflect the broader challenges of confronting historical narratives and ethical dilemmas. The Church's engagement with these issues will play a crucial role in shaping its legacy and its relationship with diverse communities in the contemporary

Conclusion

Recap of the Vatican's Diplomatic Challenges During WWII

The Vatican's diplomatic challenges during World War II were multifaceted and deeply rooted in a complex interplay of moral, political, and humanitarian considerations. As the war unfolded, the Vatican found itself navigating a treacherous landscape marked by totalitarian regimes, humanitarian crises, and ethical dilemmas. The election of Pope Pius XII in 1939 marked a pivotal moment, as he inherited a delicate balance of maintaining the Church's traditional role as a spiritual authority while responding to the pressing moral imperatives of the time.

One of the most significant challenges faced by the Vatican was its commitment to neutrality amidst a backdrop of global conflict. The Church sought to maintain its position as a mediator between belligerent powers while advocating for peace and diplomacy. This approach, however, was met with criticism and skepticism, particularly regarding the perceived silence of Pope Pius XII in the face of the Holocaust and Nazi atrocities. The complexities of balancing diplomatic relations with both Axis and Allied powers created a moral quagmire that tested the Church's integrity and commitment to its ethical principles.

Moreover, the Vatican's engagement with fascist regimes in Italy and Germany posed additional challenges. The Church faced pressure to protect its interests while navigating the dangers posed by totalitarianism. The moral complexities of these relationships raised profound questions about the Church's responsibilities in the face of grave injustices. The Vatican's efforts to shelter victims, such as Jews fleeing persecution, were often overshadowed by its diplomatic considerations and concerns about its position in a rapidly changing political landscape.

As the war progressed, the Vatican's involvement in secret peace talks and its attempts to mediate between conflicting parties illustrated the Church's desire to contribute positively to the resolution of global conflicts. However, these efforts were often met with challenges stemming from mistrust, conflicting interests, and the realities of a world torn apart by war.

In summary, the Vatican's diplomatic challenges during World War II were characterized by a constant struggle to navigate the complexities of neutrality, moral responsibility, and the quest for peace. The decisions made during this period continue to resonate in contemporary discussions about the Church's role in international relations and its moral obligations in times of crisis.

Reflection on the Moral Complexities of the Vatican's Actions

The actions of the Vatican during World War II present a rich tapestry of moral complexities that continue to evoke debate and reflection. The choices made by Church leaders in response to the unfolding atrocities reveal a struggle between the imperatives of compassion and the harsh realities of political diplomacy.

One of the most pressing moral dilemmas faced by the Vatican was the question of silence. Pope Pius XII's decision to refrain from publicly condemning Nazi atrocities has been a focal point of criticism, raising concerns about complicity and moral cowardice. While some argue that his silence was a strategic move to protect the Church and its followers from retribution, others contend that it represented a failure to stand against evil at a critical moment. The moral implications of choosing caution over vocal condemnation continue to provoke deep ethical discussions about the responsibilities of leaders in positions of authority.

Additionally, the Vatican's engagement with fascist regimes raises questions about the ethical responsibilities of institutions when confronted with oppressive systems. The moral complexities of balancing self-preservation with advocacy for human rights highlight the challenges faced by organizations operating within repressive political environments. The decisions made during this period prompt a reevaluation of how religious institutions should navigate the interplay between faith, ethics, and political realities.

The actions taken by individual clergy members during the war, including efforts to shelter refugees and provide assistance to victims, illustrate the potential for moral agency within institutional frameworks. While the Vatican's overarching policies may have been fraught with complexity, the compassion and bravery demonstrated by many Church officials serve as a testament to the capacity for individual moral courage in the face of adversity.

In conclusion, the moral complexities of the Vatican's actions during World War II serve as a reminder of the challenging ethical landscape faced by institutions and leaders in times of crisis. The reflections on this period urge contemporary leaders to grapple with the moral imperatives of their decisions and the impact of those choices on the lives of individuals and communities.

Lessons Learned from Vatican Diplomacy for Future Conflicts

The lessons learned from Vatican diplomacy during World War II provide valuable insights for contemporary leaders and institutions navigating the complexities of global conflicts. The experiences of the Vatican during this tumultuous period underscore the importance of ethical considerations, transparency, and a commitment to human rights in diplomatic engagements.

One of the key lessons is the necessity of vocal condemnation against injustice. The experience of the Vatican during the war highlights the moral imperative for leaders to take a clear stand against atrocities, particularly when lives are at stake. Silence in the face of evil can be interpreted as complicity, and contemporary leaders must recognize the significance of their voices in advocating for justice and human dignity.

Additionally, the Vatican's efforts to mediate peace underscore the importance of diplomacy in resolving conflicts. The lessons learned from the Vatican's attempts at negotiation remind us that dialogue and collaboration can be powerful tools for promoting understanding and reconciliation. In a world often divided by conflict, the commitment to diplomatic solutions remains essential for fostering a culture of peace.

The experiences of individual clergy members who acted courageously to protect victims during WWII also serve as a reminder of the potential for moral agency within institutions. Encouraging and empowering individuals within organizations to speak out against injustice and take action can create a ripple effect that promotes a culture of compassion and accountability.

Furthermore, the challenges faced by the Vatican in maintaining neutrality highlight the complexities of navigating ethical considerations in global politics. Leaders must be aware of the delicate balance between advocacy and diplomacy, ensuring that their actions align with their moral principles while seeking to address the pressing needs of those affected by conflict.

In conclusion, the lessons learned from Vatican diplomacy during World War II offer valuable guidance for contemporary leaders. The commitment to vocal advocacy, the importance of diplomatic engagement, the potential for individual moral courage, and the need for ethical decision-making are essential elements that can inform future approaches to conflict resolution and human rights advocacy.